Raven
Quill

i

CHILDREN
OF IRIS:
REBORN

by:
Raven Quill
&
Draeden Quill

CHILDREN OF IRIS:
REBORN

Proof Productions
Karnack, TX 75661
@2016 by Jeff Brannon

Printed in the USA.
ISBN-13: 978-1511944281
ISBN-10: 1511944285

Cover illustration by Proof Productions.

Children of Iris: Reborn is a work of fiction. While many of the subjects are real, all of the characters, places, and depiction of events are the products of the authors' imagination or are used fictitiously. Any mention of brand names, places, and trademarks remain the property of their respective owners, bear no association with the author or publisher, and are used for fictional purposes only. Any resemblance to actual events, locales, person, or persons, living or dead is entirely coincidental.

Dedication:

To all our family and friends who have believed in us and encouraged us to always move forward.

Acknowledgements:

We extend our humblest thanks to Rachael, Jeff and
Jasmine:
For loaning us your time and talents, and without whom
we never would have
kept the attention span to finish.

Per mortem vita

---------- **Prologue** ----------

Martin's footsteps echoed through the narrow corridors, making the already cramped spaces feel more like a dungeon than an underwater lab. His military formal wear clashed with the off-white walls surrounding him. He shifted the briefcase he was carrying from one hand to the other. This place made him uneasy. Looking through the windows sparsely placed along the walkways was all but useless. At almost 5 miles below the surface of the ocean light was artificially cast to the surrounding area, though nothing of interest ever came within range of its beams. Martin wondered if the collection of scientists living here had actually come up with anything over the past 6 months. To think of even half of the things they had conceived down here already would require insanity of which caliber only exists in comic books.

The last time here, he recalled, they had shown him a device which literally shook atoms. At first, the concept sounded as useless as a spork, but then they passed an apple into a locked safe without compromising the atomic structure of either. Currently, the Department of

Defense is working on grenades that can pass through walls. Hopefully they will be successful in creating a fully functioning prototype within the next 7 years.

Stopping at an intersection, he had to read the signs posted to find Exhibit Room C. Turning right he continued, it didn't take long before the sounds of people murmuring in excitement pervaded the air. Having already passed several security checkpoints he wasn't surprised to be stopped again at the door. After showing his I.D., handing over his briefcase, and having to step through yet another scanner, he was allowed access to his final destination.

The room smelled of bleach and looked as though the seating arrangements were an afterthought. All eight of the observers who were in conversation hushed as he entered the room. This was the man they had all been waiting for and soon the show-and-tell would begin.

"Do my eyes deceive me or is this Mr. Shore I see before us?" A tall blonde-haired man stood beside a white screen hiding the few devices they would show today. A soft humming emanated from behind it coupled with random electrical flashes.

"It's General Shore, Mr. Adams." Martin stated for the umpteenth time.

"Yes of course, my apologies, General."

Stephen Adams had a way of acting for the cameras even when they weren't around. He had an air of arrogance mixed with sarcastic intelligence, the likes of which made for a better politician than a scientist. Yet here he stood, a full-fledged PhD in biochemistry and a masters in physics, at the ripe young age of 32. Stephen joined the project only 3 years before and had quickly risen to be the Head of Operations through sheer skill and innovation.

"What have you got for me today Director?" Martin wanted to get out of there as fast as possible. Based on what he'd seen in the past, the possibility of something melting or going nuclear grew with each passing second and he didn't want to be here when someone poured the wrong liquid into the wrong vial. Smiling like a child with a secret, he ushered Martin toward a seat. "Now, now, Mr. General Shore, are you going to ruin the only fun I get to have every six months? Sit back and prepare to have your mind blown." He turned without waiting for a response to finish the preparations.

After a minute or two one of the security guards returned Martin's briefcase having finished their systems check of the computer which it contained. The General immediately began setting up a camera and booting up his computer. Several minutes later the preparations were complete and the General was streaming live to his commanding officer. With a thumbs up signal, Mr. Adams was ready to begin.

"Ladies and Gentlemen, and possibly aliens or even clones from the future," he winked at the camera, getting a snicker or two from his colleagues, "I am proud to present to you three new items to assist in the evolution of mankind worldwide." A small table was rolled forward covered by a tablecloth. Stray wires and a metal plate stuck out from the otherwise lumpy sheet. "First I must give credit where credit is due. While we have three items to show today, the first two are derived from the same project." He motioned to a man a few rows behind Martin. "Elric, the head of Project Dead Weight, has made several breakthroughs, and as a result, his team has several new inventions to work on. Give him a hand everybody." Claps, whistles, and cheers came from the few energetic people in the room.

"So without further ado, I give you..." pulling off the tablecloth, he revealed a small plate no more than 6 inches in diameter floating above the table. "... the anti-gravity plate!" Several in the crowd were shocked while a couple of guys high-fived over their success. Mr. Shore moved the table beneath the plate and waved his hands all around the disk like he was doing a magic trick. Though he did surprise everyone when he threw it like a frisbee across the room to a shocked scientist, who was barely able to catch it in time. "Elric and his team made a few major discoveries in time-space theories as well as application." He motioned for the scientist to throw the disk back. Upon catching it he flipped the disk upside down and dropped it, letting it fall to the floor with a metallic clang. "Notice the disk is only anti-gravity with the correct polarization and doesn't increase gravity on the opposing side." Satisfied he had shown just enough to pique interest, he put the disk back on the table. "Take note that currently we can only make it for specific intensities to remain at a very specific height in relation to the earth, but we're working on an adjustable version." He took a bow as several people clapped.

Two men rolled forward a medium-sized table and removed its tablecloth. On the table sat a machine as colorful and oddly shaped as anything Willy Wonka could have created. In the very center was the only recognizable part. A gyro with colored, multiple hues of blue and purple, slowly rotated. "Now," Director Adams had obviously rehearsed, "for those of us that can never get the temperature just right." He let the last word hang in the air. "Using the same theories for the anti-gravity disk, Elric's team made another discovery involving something scientists worldwide have been trying to achieve for decades." Stephen flipped a few switches and the gyro began moving faster and faster until it was nothing more than a smoky mist of color. At the center a solid mass began to take shape in a perfect sphere.

Martin gawked at the creation of what looked to be glass or ice but had no idea whatsoever as to what it was. With perfect timing the Director chimed in. "Elric's team discovered that the key to Absolute Zero is not actually temperature, but the problem is the excitement of particles. To counter this, they create an immense gravitational pull in the center of the gyro sphere, while simultaneously using the gyro itself to protect against outside particles bombarding this zero-state." With a few more switches, the spinning of the machine slowed and the hovering, solid mass quickly melted into a pool of fluid, sending a tiny smoke trail into the air.

The table was quickly covered again and rolled out of the way. "Now what you have seen so far have been major scientific achievements and yet what I am about to show you will be the best of all." Martin sat forward, for once the Director didn't sound like he was just blowing smoke. Stephen walked over to the changing screen at the back of the room and slid it aside revealing a man gagged and strapped to a chair. Martin was confused, though he had seen experiments on humans here before, never had they been gagged. Not only that, but this wasn't a volunteer from the lab. This had to be one of the inmates sentenced to death row that the lab had been using to experiment on. Mr. Shore was on the verge of saying something but held his tongue realizing his CO was watching and he was not about to make a fool of himself.

The man bound in the chair appeared to be dead, showing no signs of even breathing. Although gagged, there was no telling what was about to happen. Mr. Adams said nothing, no big display of overly dramatic movements. He simply started working as though no one was watching. A small tray was wheeled next to the man containing what appeared to be a full set of surgery tools with the addition of a meat cleaver. Martin's stomach was turning already and nothing had even occurred yet. The man's left arm was unbound and stretched out over a solid wooden block where it was strapped down yet again. An I.V. had already been hooked into the man's other arm. Director Adams took a deep breath, "Wake him"

"Ladies and gentlemen I must forewarn you, if any of you have weak stomachs at all please leave or close your eyes. This will be hard to watch." He waited a moment. The room was dead silent. The bound man's eyes cracked open, he looked around as though he were still half asleep. Adams picked up the cleaver. Eyes flying wide open, the man pulled at his bindings, suddenly well aware of what was happening. Martin gripped at the arms of his chair, the room was silent save for the struggling man. "Hold him!" Adams shouted to his partner. The other man obeyed, doing his best to hold the man down. Adams' brought the blade down with a sickening crack as it made its way into the poor man's wrist. Though gagged, his screams couldn't be muffled.

Mr. Adams pried the cleaver from the bone and brought the knife down again, this time fully severing the hand from the arm with a sickening thud. "Do it!" He shouted to his assistant as both men rushed to the syringes. The Director put his in first, emptying the contents into the still screaming and thrashing man's arm. The assistant emptied his into the I.V. seconds after. The man's screams faded after a moment and he fell unconscious again.

Shakily, Mr. Adams returned his tools to the tray leaving the hand where it lay. Blood poured from the open wrist and pooled onto the white tile. The Director took a moment to recollect himself before he continued. "Ladies and Gentlemen I'm sorry you had to see that but it was the only way to prove this works. What we are about to show you is derived from Project Iris. Originally the goal was to create a virus capable of targeting specific individuals while remaining harmless to others exposed to the virus. Our first problem was the task of marking a target. How could a virus know who is or isn't the target without us directly injecting it into the subject?" Everyone was still in a slight daze from the horrific sight they just beheld. Martin was glad to notice the bleeding had slowed; he didn't want the man to die like this, regardless of his crimes. Stephen continued, trying to wipe away the blood from his shirt. "Our first answer was to give the virus a mind. That way all we had to do was tell the virus what the target was. Well, after a while we realized that creating a brain on such a small scale was close to impossible. Then we thought 'Why not hack the human brain?'." He paused for effect, slowly regaining composure and confidence. "Well, I'm here before you today to tell you today that is exactly what we've done! In doing so, we have discovered entirely new ways of healing the body." The bleeding came to a full stop and Martin released his held breath, forgetting the last time he inhaled. "Cancer, AIDS, blindness, Alzheimer's, migraines, and even lost limbs can all be cured through the mind with the help of Iris."

A girl at the front pointed to the man's wounded arm, "Oh my God!" she gasped. The room's attention turned to the bound man's arm. A tendril of muscle worked its way from the wound like a worm writhing on a hook. A second segment appeared, followed by a third, all seeming to grow from the man's arm. The bone started to extend and heal on its own. Muscle wrapped around bone, and flesh grew as the familiar shape of a hand began to form. Stephen continued, "Iris analyzes short-term memory and stays dormant for up to 72-hours in the brain. We tried working with long-term memory, but it takes weeks for Iris to activate. So to be more efficient we went with short-term until we can perfect Iris." Fingers spread forth and flesh spread like butter over hot pancakes. The tint of the flesh seemed darker in comparison the the rest of the body, but then again, no one was really sure what to expect from this. "While our

9

tests have had.... varied results, I can say we have plans on making Iris capable of communication which will allow us better control, as well as an understanding on what exactly the entire process is that Iris runs through."

A bright red box appeared on Martin's computer, indicating he received a message. Reading through it quickly, he shut his computer off and began packing. Confused the Director rushed over. "I'm sorry. Do they not like this? We can repurpose it towards con-"

"It's fine," Martin interrupted. "They love them all. Continue your work on Project Dead Meat. Project Iris, however, is complete. Send everything you have to command and shut it down. Repurpose your resources until we send you the information on your new project."

"But General, didn't you hear? We can still improve on this." Martin finished packing and started walking to the door.

"Shut it down Director, that's an order from the top. We'll be handling it from now on." With that he was gone.

"Sir?" David, Stephen's assistant asked. "We aren't going to shut it down just like that are we?"

Stephen laughed like he was still on camera. "No, not at all. This is too big a project to give up. I have some friends at Holy that'll work on this for me until we can get to it." He motioned to the room. "Thank you everyone for your hard work and participation today. Three extra hours of leisure time today and tomorrow. Tell your teams and enjoy your time off. You are all dismissed." Stephen turned back to his assistant. "Have them clean everything up, then afterwards I want you to make a copy of everything on Project Iris and hide it in the secure locker in my bedroom. Are we clear?"

"Y..Yes Sir!" David said hurrying out of the room but quickly popped his head back into the doorway. "Um sir... how exactly are we supposed to sneak Iris out?"

Stephen turned his back to his assistant and focused his attention on the severed hand soaked in blood.

"There's a little part I failed to mention earlier... Iris is waterborne."

Stephen couldn't take his eyes off of the blood on the floor. Something about the contrasting pure white floor and the crimson blood sent a tingling shiver up his spine.

---------- Chapter 1 ---------

"Is there anything more disheartening than a Wednesday at 12 o'clock? Dealing with 20 hours of non-stop phone calls, made by what seems to be the planet's least tech savvy citizens, makes for a long week", Guy said to the noticeably asymmetrical swan he had crafted at his desk from the scraps of office memos. "The only thing worse is knowing you have another 20 hours to go."

"I'm sorry, am I keeping you from something more important?" The voice in his ear changed from frustrated to irate. "This is ridiculous, I want to speak with a manager!"

Guy now glanced at the phone and noticed the absence of a familiar glowing light. "Sorry, I usually put anyone higher than a three on mute. I'll make sure a supervisor will call you back at their earliest convenience."

He hung up the phone. *What would she do with a smartphone anyway?* Just another user flooding the social network streams with cat pictures and quotes from old newspaper comic strips printed by Gutenberg himself. *I did the internet a favor.*

He had a system. Cheerful or even apathetic callers were a one. He could deal with those. They then went up, based on their volume and proficiency with obscenities, to a maximum of five. A one meant he would take another call, a five meant it was time to smoke.

Guy only really smoked socially, but if he could use it as an excuse to leave the building every few hours he would take it. He would sit under the pavilion designated for smokers and watch the rest of the workforce come and go. They would talk about sports (of which he had little interest), or work (of which he had even less interest), or on occasion, a new movie gracing the box office charts. He often found himself spending entire days at the cinema so he didn't mind briefly joining in on those conversations.

He had been working in customer support for the past five years. He started as a billing representative for a hearing aid company. It took him a full four days to realize that job wasn't for him. He was then hired at his current job working technical support for a small cellular phone provider. It was only because of his longevity that he hadn't been fired.

Guy browsed the break room refrigerator as he milked the last minutes of his shift. Weeks worth of expired leftovers filled the shelves, only leaving room for small beverage containers. The only thing unopened was a bottle of water someone clearly brought from home. No branding label, no name written in possessive black marker, and most importantly, none of the little brown specks floating in it like the "purified" tap water usually available to employees. He took the bottle and broke the seal as he sauntered back to his desk.

"Is that my water?" said a passing coworker. "You thieving bastard!"

"Munch me, Keith." Guy said as he took another swig from the bottle.

Only moments later, Guy emerged from the double doors of the office building as if he was an old man with a shotgun guarding his front porch. Patrons at the cafe across the street, sipping their overpriced coffees, watched in amusement. He walked to the small, two story parking garage and unlocked the door to his prized possession.

The 1969 El Camino had been his money pit since he bought it on graduation day five years ago. Nearly all the original parts had been replaced at this point, setting him back thousands of dollars, but the car's matte black and royal purple paint job was by far his favorite upgrade. Sure the gas mileage was awful and the passenger seat had a gash in the back support that he would rather not explain, but it was the only thing he owned that made him feel like an adult.

Guy made his way downtown, hitting nearly every red light and drumming on his steering wheel to his shuffled playlist. Tonight was his Noudouken Ryu class. He only joined because a friend signed them both up. The same friend who promptly quit two weeks later. Surprisingly enough, he came to enjoy his bi-weekly sessions. He was coming up on his year mark and he could actually tell a difference between himself then and now. Two more years and he would have the chance to go to competitions, if he wasn't too busy sitting at home playing games on his cell phone of course.

The dojo was a small building, having only enough room for the sparring mat and a few racks used to hold various practice weapons. On the walls hung a row of different colored belts and framed pictures of previous competition winners who used to take lessons there. As you walked through the front door you could see several chairs that were lined against the entrance wall, placed there for any friends or family who wanted to stay and watch the practice.

Alright I'm up next. I really should have stretched before this. Damn that's a big dude. I bet he could palm my head like a basketball. Guy sat and watched the sparring match between the 6'4 pile of ugly muscle that sometimes went by Greg, and the 5'6 investment broker, Jeremy. *Ouch! That couldn't have felt good. He's not*

moving. No wait, I think his eye just fluttered. 11.8
seconds. All I have to do is last 12 seconds and I'm
better than Jeremy. I mean, most bull riders only last
eight and Greg is slightly smaller than a bull.

Guy stepped into the taped circle on the floor. The signal
was given and immediately the pain started. Right away
Greg landed a left hook half an inch behind Guy's
temple. Everything went blurry. *Ah shit! Did we start?*
This is it. This is how it happens. I'm going to die here
with nothing but the ringing in my ears and the taste of
turquoise. What's that dark shadow? Dark circular
shadow? Fist? Fist. Fist! He ducked just in time to
escape a right jab and threw his knuckles up to make
connection with Greg's jaw. A cracking noise and a
burning sensation shot up Guy's wrist. He reeled his arm
back and looked up just in time to watch one of Greg's
teeth soar into the empty guest seating area. Greg also
noticed his now aerial tooth and turned glaring in Guy's
direction. One punch to the shoulder sent Guy face first
onto the ground.

The Sensei stepped in to pull Greg back but was shoved
onto the ground as Greg jumped onto Guy's back. In one
swoop he turned Guy around and proceeded to pound
his face to mush until four of the other students managed
to pull him off.

The Sensei ran to the battered pulp lying motionless on the floor and called for his other students to bring ice and the first aid kit. With his eyes open as wide as he could manage, Guy watched as his mentor fashioned an ice pack out of the ice and layers of paper towels. He took the offered compress and brought himself to a sitting position. He watched as interest in his wounds faded and people started to leave.

"None of the cuts are deep enough for stitches," Sensei said as Guy stood up to gather his things. "I am sorry though. I was not expecting Greg to continue fighting so vigorously. I lost my footing."

"It's not your fault. Who would have guessed I would land a lucky shot that would send Goliath into a rampage?"

Guy bowed to his teacher and walked out of the building. It was dark now and had been for about an hour. *Phone, wallet, pen, keys. Wait where are my keys?* Guy looked behind him to see that his dojo was now two blocks away and empty.

Are you shitting me? He was now close enough to slam his fist onto the roof of his car. With his head resting on the driver's window he saw his keys lying on the center console. *Well that solves one problem.*

17

After numerous attempts at pulling on the door handle, Guy swallowed his pride and reached for his phone. He and his ex didn't part on the best of terms, but he hoped that, after explaining the day he had, she would find it in her cold, black heart to bring him his only spare set of keys. He knew, in hindsight, he should have taken them back when he had the chance. *No answer. Of course she wouldn't answer. If I was busy sleeping with everyone in town I wouldn't answer either.*

Guy and Lindsey had dated off and on since high school, but even back then he had a hard time coming up with a reason to like her. Sure she was pretty, but one good quality couldn't mask the dozens of things he simply couldn't stand. She was the kind of girl who spent her life on her phone posting pictures to social media. The kind of girl who thought Biology was the study of bisexual people. After soul searching, Guy simply realized he had nothing better to do.

Just as he was putting his phone away, he was spun around and pinned to his car, sending the phone crashing into the ground and bouncing under the vehicle. Three men with baseball bats had formed a half-circle around him, one of which had his hand pincered around Guy's neck. No thoughts came to him as they threw him to the ground. His brain pounded against the side of his skull as his head bounced off the concrete. He was unconscious only long enough not to notice the attackers taking everything from his pockets. Waking up in a haze, he tried to scramble away. One swift kick to his ribs quickly ended that, however, and sent him rolling over onto his back.

The next few moments seemed to take a lifetime, though they happened too fast to avoid. Every few seconds, wooden baseball bats came down hard onto his chest and legs. Quickly the pain became too much, and he couldn't feel anything at all, but he could still hear the tearing of his skin and the snapping of his bones. One of them mumbling about being recognized later was the last sound he heard that night. Colors all blended together, but he could make out the outline of one the muggers standing over him, bat held high overhead. It came down hard with a sickening crack. Lying there in the blackness, Guy felt his heart beat one more time, then nothing.

---------- Chapter 2 ----------

Luke Jones was born with a plastic spoon in his mouth. That is to say he was destined for mediocrity, a life filled with vast open fields of boredom and monotony. Even his name was comprised with two of the most common male names in America. At 5'7" and a thin build he hardly stood out of a crowd. His light brown hair served more to hide him than to appear unique. This however, didn't stop him from striving to be something more. Since childhood Luke could only dream of being a hero.

In grade school he would dress in costume and tell all of his classmates of the super powers he'd have and how he'd save the world. As he grew older his visions turned to modern day heroes. Police officer, firefighter, monk, doctor, lawyer, priest... all were within the grasp of wide-eyed, innocent Luke.

College life was actually pretty easy. He never had trouble understanding the subjects but he never had enough drive to study. An average of a B got him through his entire school career up to this point; no reason to fix what isn't broken. More recently, he had been considering dropping out. He hand no real major he was focusing on nor a career path picked out. The college path just seemed *normal,* like that was what everyone was supposed to do. He got a job, moved into his own place, and went to school. While not overly excited about his life, he would describe himself as content.

Luke would be the first to tell you his life came with its own struggles. Everything he owned he payed for out of his own pocket. Though coming from a less than average income home, he was able to appreciate life a little more than most. That combined with his dreams made him more accepting of all walks of life. His biggest fault (in his opinion) would be his apathy. While Luke had passions and dreams, he could never quite put them into action. He was a dreamer, nothing more, and he knew it.

His morals and virtues applied only in his mind. The days of heroes and quests were long since gone and no matter how much he dreamed, he would never find his own dragon to slay, a damsel to save, or evil to smite. His life would forever be eclipsed in the ever growing shadow of his own average existence.

This all quickly passed through his mind as he sat in a plain hoodie and jeans, drinking a bottle of water, leaning against a tree. Watching passively, his girlfriend's party played out in front of him like a sitcom. A BYOB sort of event where it seemed everyone was self-invited. The party wasn't supposed to be this big, a few friends at the park and a few drinks and laughter was too much to ask for apparently.

With the clouds heavy and growing darker, rain would come in droves at any moment. As was so common with a Texas fall. That didn't stop dozens of strangers from crashing the party to show their wild side. *Sarah seems to be sleeping with Kevin, though neither of them want to admit it. I would put money on David being high right now.* This was one of his favorite games. He would watch everything from a distance and try to "Sherlock Holmes" everyone. He was more often right than wrong but who's counting. A hand gripped his shoulder.

"Whatcha doin party pooper?"

It was Anastasia (Anna to friends), his girlfriend of four years. They couldn't have been more different. She being outgoing, talkative, pretty, and smart. Him, the blandest of the bland. His only saving grace was his sharp intellect and problem solving, which did him little good in social settings.

"Just watching," He said, kissing her cheek. "Enjoying the party?"

"I think I'm getting tipsy," she said coyly, kissing him back. "But the night's just started and so have I!"

She bounced away like a kitten on a mission to destroy the curtains. *How did I even get someone as beautiful and energetic as her?* He finished off his water and decided to "mingle" with her friends. Though he wasn't a fan of the party lifestyle Anna was so partial to, the social aspects in particular, he always made the attempt to be the outgoing boyfriend she so often asked him to be.

The party continued as various twenty-somethings showed up, more to drink and hook up, than to celebrate a birthday. Luke, now in the midst of the crowd, searched for Derek, his best friend. Derek and Luke grew up together living only a few houses apart and having almost all their school lives in the same classes. The old adage "opposites attract" has never had a truer example. Much like Anna, Derek was outgoing, energetic, and an ass more often than not. Here lately, the two hadn't seen much of each other. Though Luke blamed himself for this, he knew it wasn't all his fault. Being a homebody, he wasn't prone to "hanging out".

Derek had two henchmen, as Luke called them, (for lack of a more accurate term) the likes of which followed everything Derek did much like sibling emulation. If Derek asked them to jump from a bridge, Luke was certain neither had the mental faculties to resist the request. Bill and Seth were quite possibly the two dumbest human beings to walk the face of the earth.

"Bullett!" Derek shouted wading through the crowd, snapping him out of his stupor. "Where've you been?"

Bullett was Luke's nickname since middle school. He was very adept at military shooting games, and when someone is killed enough by you they learn your name.

"What's up man?" The two shared an elaborate handshake made up years ago.
"What are you doing just wandering around?"

"Well you know…" He gestured to the crowd of strangers. "socializing."

Derek laughed, walking with Luke towards the table of various alcoholic beverages. "So haven't seen you in a while, what've you been up to?"

"Same stuff as always, just kinda doing whatever passes the time." Luke said eyeing a bottle of Guinness.

"Bullett how many times have I told you this shit; you can't be so passive. Be involved in your own life. If you see something you want, take it! And when you take it, it belongs to you. If you want it bad enough, absolutely nothing will stand in your way."

Luke just nodded in agreement. Derek had the older brother tone in his voice and Luke knew better than to protest. *But there isn't anything I want. At least nothing worth risking anything over.* With Derek still staring, Luke opened his mouth as if to say something then turned and grabbed a beer instead. **THUD.** Derek's hand hit the table dramatically. Looking down, Luke noticed a large knife in the shape of a cross.

"You like?" Derek, beaming, twirled it around with finesse. "I bought this pretty baby last week, cost almost 300 dollars but it'll cut through your fucking head in a heartbeat."

With a grand display, much like Billy the Kid, he sheathed the knife in a holster on his belt. With a nod of approval, Luke started downing his own drink. Not to be outdone, Derek raced to the bottom of his own beer.

The party continued as the sun disappeared behind the thickening clouds. Thunder rolled in the distance while droplets of cold water began to sprinkle the area. The crowds thinned as more and more people left before the weather could, quite literally, rain on their parade. Even more disappeared as they found someone to sleep with for the night.

The few people remaining were either too drunk to care or friends of Anna. Luke wasn't too concerned as he lived only a few minutes of walking distance straight through the woods. With the "social" aspect becoming less social, Luke became less and less of a recluse. He proceeded to dance with Anna, joked with Derek, and even had a drinking contest with one of Derek's friends.

This however was cut short as nature couldn't contain itself any longer.

Running to the only covered sitting area, the fifteen or so people left huddled together. "Guess this means the party's over," Anna said with a mixture of humor and disappointment.

"Well, we made it last as long as we could." Laughed Bill, who had shown up at some point. If he arrived then surely Seth wouldn't be far.

"Shut up fucker, we can still drink in the rain." *Annnnd there he is. The drunkest with the least brain cells to risk losing. How the hell does anyone stand them?*

As if to enforce his point, the group as a collective toasts with whatever drinks they're holding and the drinking continues. *I'm done, I can't be around this much stupid all at once.* With that Luke elbowed his way to Anna.

"Babe! I'm drunk!" Anna wraps her arms around him. Her speech remarkably understandable, though her balance left a lot to be desired. She hangs from Luke, using him as a support while trying to sway. "This is such a great day! I'm glad you came."

This is why I don't get drunk. The question now is how do I convince her to let me leave without making her sad. "I see that. I'm buzzing pretty good too."

She tilts her head, still swinging from him. "You need to drink moooorrre."

"I'm getting a bad headache Anna, would you mind if I went and took a nap?"

"Aw is my cutie-wootie feeling bad?" *I hate her baby talk. And she only does it when she's drunk. Someday I'm gonna find a way to fix that.*

"Yeah, I figure I can just head to the house for like 30 minutes and take a quick nap. But just in case I can see if Derek can take you home." Anna pouts giving her best quivering puppy lip.

Derek walks up dripping wet. "What's up?"

Luke looks him over. "What did you do, jump in a lake?"

"Close enough. I ran out to put my stuff in the truck." Derek shook his hair like a dog fresh from a bath.

"Getting ready to leave? Would you mind taking Anna home for me? I'm getting ready to walk to the house myself." Luke secretly pleaded in his mind he would see his discomfort.

Derek looked them both over judging the situation. "I don't see why not, she's on the way anyways. You may be a bit squished, I have Bill and Seth riding with me."

Seth, who was vomiting tequila shots in a puddle, gives a thumbs up. *Thank God I don't have to be around those guys much longer.* Anna pulls Luke close and whispers into his ear.

"Come by my house after your nap, we should party alone." With a wink and quick kiss she turned to say goodbye to the rest of the group. Only a handful remained as the rest decided to get out before the weather turned worse. The thunder had been getting progressively worse as the heart of the storm grew ever closer.

After saying his own goodbyes Luke turned to Derek. "I'm gonna go ahead and go before it get's too bad."

Derek patted him on the back. "No worries man. Leave everything to me. Just be sure you make it home in one piece."

Anna was already stumbling to the truck in the parking lot. Seth danced in circles in the rain while Bill stoically stared at a bench. Looking from them to Derek, Luke can't help but shrug and laugh as he turns to trek his way home.

With his hood pulled up and hands in his pockets, Luke trudged through the thickening mud. Prepared for the walk ahead, his headphones pulsed with some random electro song his phone suggested. The fall winds, coupled with the heavy rain, made for a colder walk than expected. The trees did little to prevent the large droplets from peppering Luke and soaking through his hoodie.

Near the halfway point, Luke stopped at a creek that was now rushing with water. It wasn't deep enough to swim in but, slipping would land you at least chest deep in freezing water. He stepped back, gearing up to try to clear it. The trance-like music setting for an epic drop in time with an epic jump (at least in his mind).

Luke dashed towards the flowing water; he bent at the knee preparing to jump. Just before his giant leap an excruciating pain entered his back, followed by one in his ribs and another in his leg. His vision became hazy as the water rose to meet him in an icy embrace. No thoughts could contain his immense pain, a mixture of ice and blood, he partially sank face-first down the creek in a state of shock.

Blackness surrounded him. *Where am I? What was I doing? Did… did I die? Just like that? No chance, I just get struck by lightning or some falling tree and just like that I die. Is dying in battle too much to ask? Going out a hero, or at least putting up a fight would be nice. I haven't really lived, I mean… I haven't had my adventure. I wanted to make a difference in the world, I wanted to save people but no, I have to go and die.. die? Am I dead? I would think death would be more than this. I'm floating... sideways. Why? My chest hurts, am I breathing? I need air. I need air!*

Gasping, Luke surfaced sputtering water. Eyes still blurry, he grasped for anything within reach. Gripping at what felt like a soggy mixture of mud and leaves, he pulled himself forward. His lower half numb from either pain or the cold, neither of which being a good thing. He clawed through the mud dragging himself completely out of the rushing water struggling for breath. Choking, he coughed up a mixture of blood and water onto the already soaked earth.

Dragging himself through his own blood, struggling to make out the blurry images in front of him, he managed to find a large tree, rotted and hollow at the base. He pulled himself into the base getting what reprieve from the rain he could. Doing his best to scrunch into a seated position he surveyed his body. A large gash in his ribs pouring blood and another in his leg caked with mud and leaves. *What the hell happened? Did an animal attack me?* He reached to the source of pain in the center of his back to fully assess his damage. A large protrusion stuck out from the base of his back. Gripping it he could feel it move against his innards.

It's deep… real deep. I don't think it hit the spine but if i'm not careful... well… chances are I'm a dead man already. I think my lung is collapsed, I can barely breathe and I'm pretty sure whatever's in my back ruptured organs. Do I leave it in or take it out? I remember seeing something on tv about it but I can't remember the answer. Well as close as it is to the spine I might as well take it out. As things are now it won't really make a difference.

Pulling at it he could feel it tear and rip it's way out bringing chunks of flesh with it. The outer lining of his vision faded along with his energy. The protrusion scraped against bone leaving a permanent mark of it's passing. A wave of confusion and fear passed over Luke as he brought the bringer of his likely death into view. His consciousness waned.

A knife in his hand, covered in his own blood, stared back at him. An intricate weave of metal he had seen before now tainted by his life-giving blood. His body rocked, unable to keep himself upright, he leaned against the inside of the trunk. *There's no way… this has to be a dream… and I'm so tired.* Unable to form a complete thought, he simply stared at the blood covered knife. The rain, a static lullaby, ushers him towards the black void once more.

---------- Chapter 3 ----------

"Kid! Hey kid are you ok? Can you hear me?"

He hated being called "kid". He tried opening his eyes but the beaming light forced them to stay closed. "Yeah, yeah I'm ok." But was he? Guy took a minute to analyze the situation. *I'm not at home. My carpet is much softer than this. I must be outside but why?* The events of the night before started ebbing back into his mind. *What the hell happened to me? I was attacked. They beat me unconscious. I was dead. I felt everything shut down. But, then, why don't I feel dead?*

He opened his eyes and the silhouette of a man started coming into focus. It was a police officer. One he had seen several times before around town. He apparently didn't think Guy's answer was quite good enough as he still wore the look of anticipation.

"Y..Yeah I'm ok. Too much of the drink I guess." Guy said to deflect further questions. "Sorry officer, it won't happen again."

The officer stood to his feet and only said, "See that it doesn't." as he turned and walked away.

Guy picked himself up and started patting himself up and down. *Nothing seems to be broken.* He rolled up his sleeves. *No bruises either. What the hell is going on?* He took a few careful steps forward. *It's not like I could have been dreaming; I woke up outside!* He looked around to regain his bearings and saw his dojo across the street in front of him. He had been moved.

He started walking back to the nearly hidden parking lot he always parked in during his classes. Out of the corner of his eye he noticed his reflection in the shop windows. Everything was normal aside from the deep orange color his shirt now was. *I don't own an orange shirt. Is this blood? It takes a while for blood to dry this color. How long was I there?* Dissatisfied with any answers he could give himself, he started back towards his car. As he turned the corner around the back of the building his eyes were immediately pulled toward the deeply stained concrete around his vehicle. He walked up to the car and pulled the handle out of habit, simultaneously seeing his keys still resting on the console.

Guy sat down and leaned against his driver's side door. Once he was still, he noticed that he felt different. The kind of different that someone might feel after having one too many energy drinks. It was as if he could feel each of his muscles tighten around their respective bones and pull their corresponding tendons with even the slightest of movements he made. It finally occurred to him why everything seemed so strange. For the first time in his life, he felt alive.

Head still swimming from everything that had happened, Guy stood up and jumped straight into the air. He couldn't remember being able to jump that high. He ran across the lot and jumped again, this time easily clearing the trash bin placed there by the city for passersby. *This is insane!* He sprinted back the way he came and lept into the air, spinning horizontally over his El Camino, and landed as easily as if he had simply stepped out of the car. He looked around to see if anyone noticed his feat. Energy surged through his veins, as if the more he used, the more he gained in return.

He turned around and once again noticed his keys, still held captive. *Dammit!* In a mixture of frustration and confusion, he threw his fist at the frame of his passenger door. As the punch made connection, the two panes of glass closest to the impact point instantly spider webbed and shattered, sending glass chips flying in all directions.

What the hell did I just do? I didn't even hit it that hard! He noticed a dent in the door the size of a softball. After a few moments of pause, Guy reached in and grabbed his keys and climbed into his driver's seat. He started his car and was about to drive off when he remembered his cell. Still sitting in his seat, he leaned down to see the phone still lying where it dropped. He reached and scooped it up, tossed it into the glovebox, and drove. He wasn't quite sure where he was going, he just knew he had to get out of the city for some air.

After driving for about forty-five minutes, he pulled off the road near the thickest wooded area he could find. He walked deeper into the trees until the road was nothing more than a grey speck through the leaves. Taking a deep breath, he cracked his knuckles and sprinted toward the large tree trunk in front of him. Just before Guy would have slammed face first into the bark, he kicked off the trunk like a springboard and launched himself up toward the branch above him. In one fluid motion he took hold of the branch and used the momentum to swing into the air toward the next closest tree. Repeating those steps, he found himself at the top of one of the highest trees in the area, acres away from where he began. Energy was surging through him like voltage through a car battery.

From where he stood, Guy could see for miles in every direction. He could even see the outskirts of his small home town. He had lived there his entire life. In fact, with the exception of one very brief and hard to remember trip to Nevada, he had never left Texas. A country boy who loved the big city.

He scanned the area and quickly noticed he wasn't alone. Several men in dark grey suits were heading his direction through the dense forest. He climbed lower to get a closer look when something whizzed past his head, missing by inches. He dropped from his current perch and vaulted from one tree to the next, the sound of a dozen pairs of feet echoing after him. He dropped onto the ground and continued to run, spinning in between trees, all the while dodging the barrage of projectiles.

It didn't take Guy long to realize he was being surrounded. No matter where he ran, his hunters seemed to be right on his heels. He looked behind him and before he could turn around again, his foot sunk into a hole and he stumbled forward. As he was regaining his balance, he felt something hit and sink deep into his shoulder. Guy began to lose speed, suddenly growing tired from all the effort. *Tranquilizer darts? Really? Who the hell uses tranq darts?* He fought the toxins back, but it was too late. The mysterious strangers, all holding what looked to be pistols, had formed a tighter circle around him. He was trapped. A few more shots fired, and though he managed to avoid most of them, two drove into his skin. He could reach out and grab his attackers now.

Punching at the closest, he could feel his enemy's jaw crack and give way as his fist followed through. The man in grey fell into the grass clutching his chin. Three others ran forward and grabbed his arms, trying to restrain him. He was able to break his left arm free and couldn't help but show a smile when another of the men's noses shattered into a spray of blood.

Poison darts seemed to rain from the guns and this time he was too sluggish to avoid them. Without looking down, he counted the needles. *16. Not bad. Not bad at all...* After a few moments of trying to resist, he collapsed.

Several times he found himself waking up to vibrations, only to hear the sound of an engine and slip back into unconsciousness.

---------- **Chapter 4** ----------

Leaves and twigs gave way, making a soggy crunch underfoot. The sound echoed through the trees and bombarded Luke like a hail of bullets. Half-asleep, with a hangover sent by Hades himself, the sounds assaulted his senses in force. Groggily he sat up, slamming his head on the tree's innards, causing dust and wood to cover him. *What the hell? Where am I? What happened last night? I must have partied pretty hard.*

He analyzed his surroundings, noticing the tree encasing him right away. *Wow I partied REALLY hard. Wonder where I am.* He rolled to leave his encampment and was stopped in his tracks by a jolting pain shooting through his entire being. The electric shock of pain sent him into a fetal position as his skin and muscles ripped with every little motion.

In a moment of pure and unfiltered pain, his mind reached a state of clarity. The sensation of his entire body feeling as though it were falling apart brought back the memories of the previous night. The sound of footsteps approaching echoed in his ears in a sickening way. Everything combined into the heralding of his imminent death. Doing his best to ignore the pain, he slid himself back into his hiding spot, trying to not cry out in agony.

Once inside, he pulled the nearby pine straw and leaves up to create a small barrier. He steadied his breath as best as he could. He paused and took a deep breath. *I thought I lost a lung last night? Did I over analyze everything?* He looked to his wounds. *They... they're almost fully closed.. how do they already have scar tissue growing? How long have I been here? Where'd the knife go?*

His thoughts were cut short as a pair of feet stopped just behind him. However, more continued further away, through the woods they became muffled but it was definitely more than one person.

"Where the hell did he go?" A voice boomed almost making Luke jump straight out of his skin.

"He couldn't have gone far." A second voice called from further away. Luke's blood froze, they sounded familiar.

"Would you two shut up! If he's still alive we don't need to scare him into hiding!" A sickening jolt ran through his spine.

Derek? Could the other two be Bill and Seth? Are they looking to help me or are they the cause of this? That

knife looked just like Derek's. Wait... where is the knife?
"

Losing his grip on reality, time and space, Luke simply stared at his empty blood-stained hand. A glimmer of metal directly in the center of his palm. It writhed like a worm burrowing into his hand. Only a wisp before it vanished, leaving no trace of ever being there.

"Hey! Over here!" The one that sounded like Seth shouted from the front this time. Luke snapped back into a more sober state. Through the pile of leaves and sticks he could see a figure near the bank of the creek. Two others joined him. "Looks like something dug into the mud here."

Luke held his breath as the three approached his hiding spot. Surely they could hear his heart from where they were now, pounding like tribal drums against his chest. *This is it. This is how it ends. This is how I go out.* All three shadows stood before him, forming a giant silhouette. Appearing as though the Grim Reaper himself stood above Luke's grave.

A pair of green and orange sneakers paced in front of him as if searching. Luke held his breath watching. *I hate those shoes, their very existence disgusts me. Like when Derek wanted to buy those same kind I spent weeks trying to talk him out of it. So... so it isn't Derek is it?*

A sickening chill made its way through every fiber of his being. A hand reached through the opening in the tree grabbing his ankle. He jerked his leg away instinctively. Unable to hold his breath he screamed, his voice dry and cracking. "Stay away from me! Please somebody help!" The hand hesitated and then retreated.

Moments passed, time being a blur with the adrenalin flowing. Luke's eyes hurt, at some point he had closed them tightly. His eyes opened with a welcoming sight, the three disappeared like vapor. The sound of nature replacing their overpowering shadows. Luke exhaled, feeling as though all the sin and weight of the world left his lungs in a single breath.

Were they ever really there or did I scare them off? Maybe they ran to get help. He flexed his hand, sensing manageable pain, he tried his other limbs. His wounds had healed enough to at least move them, however painful, he surmised it to be safe enough to crawl out making himself easier to find. He rolled onto all fours and stopped. A rustling sound from behind, too loud to be an animal just walking through the woods, creeped closer. He hadn't heard it before but now it seemed there was something approaching.

The sounds of birds chirping, squirrels prancing, and the breeze blowing all fell silent. Luke recalled seeing a documentary on wildlife having a sixth sense that alerted them to danger. *Should I hide or reveal myself? I'm not really in the open yet, maybe I should just wait for it to pass and then decide. No sense in jumping out in front of a wild dog or something bigger without knowing what it is first.*

Keeping his eyes on what little view he had available in his small space, his tension mounted once again. The rustling, very loud now, came from all sides, echoing inside the tree. It sounded like a dozen rakes gathering leaves at once. It continued to echo, forming static noise in his mind. Distance being immeasurable by anything other than sound he could only wait. Sweat formed on his brow, dripping across his eye though he was too focused to blink.

A thud hit the tree from behind followed by another, almost as if struck by a falling limb. Luke repositioned to put an ear to the tree listening. The scraping and dragging of leaves, quieter now, circled his refuge. With a final thud, a cluster of branches fell directly in front of the opening. His view now blocked, his stomach sunk, this could be nothing but an ill omen.

"Are we really gonna do this?" A voice whispered

"We're past the point of chickening out now." Replied another in a less hushed tone.

Silence followed as Luke could do nothing but bite his lip and wait. All at once the feet of the strangers pounded away in a sprint until they disappeared completely. Leaving a small popping noise in their wake. Luke suddenly realized his fate. *They're going to burn me alive!* Smoke spread into the tree like a snake twisting towards him. He pushed the limbs aside to dash out but the fire had already spread directly in front of him. Leaves and dead branches circled around the base of the tree. A few feet away an empty gas canister on its side, burned with everything around it.

Luke retreated into the tree as far as he could. The dried and rotted insides falling away to the touch. With great effort he clawed at the wood, digging as much away as he could. Fingers bleeding, he could feel the flames licking at his shoes as he tried to pry chunks of wood away. He paused, searching for some alternate method. *The knife!* He quickly searched around him unable to locate it, fire had already begun spreading to the interior parts of the tree. He didn't have time to waste. He started screaming for help as he lost precious oxygen. Luke frantically clawed and screamed, cracking and inaudible, cries for help, losing fingernails one after the other.

The flames started to crawl up his legs slowly, carefully embracing him. With energy fading and flesh ripping, he desperately begged for anyone or anything to save him.

Digging a wide enough hole to see through, his last hope for escaping faded.

On the other side, branches had been piled up just like the entrance and were already burning. He was completely trapped in an ever-growing inferno. His mind blank with his only goal survival. Fingers down to a pulp, he could do little more than punch at the wood.

"Hey!" Shouted an old man appearing behind the flames. "Hey someone help there's a guy trapped over here!" He grabbed dirt throwing it onto the burning ground trying to forge a path.

Luke, very near death, for the second time in 24 hours found his will to live. His one hope was this man. Luke pounded at the walls of his prison as the man tried to push into his burning hell; shouting things like "You're going to make it" and "I've got you." all the while. Luke felt the flames working their way to his shirt. He punched at the hole giving it everything within him.

Silver tendrils shot forth from the skin of his arm forming a hardened fist around his own. He punched into the trunk with even greater force than before, the silver coating acting as a protective gauntlet. Chunks of wood splintered away. Luke was too busy trying not to burn to death to notice the change. He continued to break away large sections until there was enough space to squeeze through. He forced his head and a single arm through, using those as leverage to push against the trunk bringing more of him through it.

The old man held his arms out over the flames ready to pull Luke through. With a great echoing sound the tree above him cracked.

"It's about to fall you have to hurry!" The old man yelled.

The trunk gave way, allowing Luke freedom to move. He jumped through the opening, legs ablaze and skin splitting, toward his saviour as the tree collapsed. Midair, he could see the tree looming above like a guillotine. Luke fell into his arms as the man rolled to protect him from the falling timber. It landed beside them throwing embers into the air to fall like burning snow. The old man quickly threw dirt over Luke's burning body. "You're gonna be ok kid just stay with me." Luke could hear him but was in no state of mind to respond. Out of stamina, he faded into unconsciousness as his hand turned back to flesh and blood once more.

---------- Chapter 5 ----------

Somewhere out in East Texas there's a small unassuming town. Everyone knows everybody's business and yet their day to day lives never change. A single movie theater and a bowling alley are the greatest forms of entertainment just slightly ahead of a dying mall with more shutters closed than open. A train station, an interstate, and several highways intersect here, yet the city seems somewhat behind the rest of the world. In one of the abandoned factory sites dotting the outskirts lies a plain brick building. Sitting just outside of the public eye, it stands five stories tall with security around the clock.

Past the three security checkpoints, through the iron doors, and up a password locked elevator, a foreboding hallway with a half-dozen locked doors on either side is only accessible by those with the highest clearance. A constant smell of chemical cleaners gave it a very hospital-like aroma. The rooms themselves all appeared as middle-class hotel rooms. Two queen-sized beds, a single desk complete with rolling chair, an alarm clock and a tube tv way past its warranty were all that were allowed to its two occupants.

Two men shared the room. One was a slender, brown-haired male in his early twenties that had just been brought here only hours before. The first to arrive had already been there for almost two weeks and had grown accustomed to his surroundings, while the second (literally kicking and screaming as he was brought in) had yet to accept his situation.

The newcomer was tossed to the floor with little regard for his wellbeing. In seconds the two were left alone with the door locking them in. "What's your name?" The first, only slightly taller than the newcomer, standing about 5'10 with dirty blonde hair, asked after his new roommate had finally calmed down enough to speak.

His mind reeled from his situation. His memories in tatters from the past few days. He could recall the party, he remembered the fire and even spending a few days in the hospital, but after that, nothing up until the moment he was being thrown into a room by strangers. Luke responded defensively using the first name he could think of that wasn't really his.

"Bullett...with two T's why? What's yours? No wait, where am I?" He stared at this bemused man. By looks they were probably around the same age, yet he didn't appear fazed by this situation.

"The Maze." Guy glanced at the time then back to Bullett

Bullett stared at him blankly. "What do you mean "The Maze"?" He tried to place a lot of sarcasm at the end but it only came out quivering and childish.

"You're weird. An oddity. I mean that in the nicest way possible. Something about you makes these guys nervous and the only way they can ease their own minds is to lay out the piece of cheese and let you run for it." Guy said without changing his expression. "We're lab rats. All we can do is look for the end of the maze. And for the record the name's Guy."

Bullett was a bit taken aback, it was uncommon to find someone with a level of communication to sum up such a foreign concept into such a specific example. Even more so, this was the first person he considered to be of equal intelligence at first introduction. *This guy is a drama queen for sure but… I kinda like this "Guy".*

"Ok, so if we're the rats in a maze, what's the cheese?" Bullett was calming down, the person in front of him had an air of confidence that felt contagious.

"That's the shittiest part of all this. There is no cheese. They tell you there is, but there isn't. It's all a game in order to get us to comply with whatever it is they want us to do. Either way, we're stuck. The doors are locked with at least three electronic locks and that's to get out of this room alone." Guy explained to his new roommate. "I'm not sure what they're looking for, but we're here until they find it."

"So what you're saying is… the cheese is a lie?" His eyebrow arched in anticipation of a response.

"Yes, it's cheesecake." Guy smirked at the joke.

"I'm glad you got that," Bullett said grinning Suddenly he remembered his situation his expression dropped. "Exactly how boned are we right now?"

"Well as far as captors go, these have actually been nicer than expected. Though we are still being held hostage, and that's never good. So on a scale of one to ten, we would get our own reality show based on the amount of boned we are."

Bullett stared at his feet. He couldn't remember buying those shoes, nor ever putting them on. He couldn't remember what he had for dinner the night before, nor what the weather was like. None of that seemed to bother him as much as it should have. Though for some reason he could remember fear. The fear he felt the night he burned haunted him. Like one long nightmare he couldn't wake up from. He clenched his fists and looked Guy in the eye.

"You have an escape plan yet?"

"My Sensei always used to tell me 'Never give the high ground to your enemy'." Guy said gesturing to random areas around the room. "It's difficult to plan when the walls have ears."

"Wait, are you saying our room is bugged? Like cameras and microphones… the whole nine yards?" He glanced around the room for all the obvious places. A few he could see from where he stood, still at the entrance. *One in the smoke detector, another in the sensor on the front of the tv and I'm pretty sure that's a mic on top of the alarm clock.*

"Let's just say if you take a slightly longer piss than normal they'll know about it and, undoubtedly, document their findings. Speaking of, the bathroom is through that door." Guy motioned toward a door near one of the beds and glanced back at the clock.

Bullett nodded, quickly looking to the clock himself. *Three O'clock but it doesn't say AM or PM so we have no way of knowing whether it's day or night.*

"Does the tv work?" He asked gesturing towards the ancient device so crass as to consider itself technology.

"If you call standard definition and only one channel "working" then yes, it works like a charm."

Bullett found it curious that a tv would be provided to people that had been kidnapped. He approached and pressed the power button. An electric sound hummed through it and he could feel the hairs on his arms stand on end near the screen. After a full two seconds (a lifetime by current standards) the screen popped up. "... victims near the station were found under the refuse. More explosions were reported near.." He turned it back off. It seemed normal enough but there's no telling what "they" were monitoring. Either way he could not stand to hear bad news at that particular moment.

"How long have you been here?" He asked Guy, noting the severely lacking items in the room.

"Today makes thirteen days," Guy said without hesitation. "Did you know that amusement parks will set their clocks to run slower than normal to make the guests think they haven't been there as long as they actually have?"

Bullett paused. *Is this guy nervous, crazy, or trying to tell me something? Probably crazy now that I look at him.* "One, what does that have to do with anything? Two, couldn't a person tell the actual time by looking at their phone and three, do they reset them every day?"

"The difference is only by milliseconds, but it's enough to add up over time. Most people assume their time is off when all the other clocks around them show the same time. All I'm saying is time is relative to the observer. Though they have thirteen days of test results with my name on them, I haven't been here quite that long if the clock is correct. Thankfully, I can count to sixty."

"Well that's a relief at least. Does the time signify anything imp…" Bullett was cut off by a loud mechanical noise coming from somewhere under the floor accompanied with an alarm ringing from the clock. "What the hell is that?" He tried shouting over the ear-splitting sound.

"It's testing time. I hope you brought a pencil." Guy smirked as he stood up. He walked over to one of the beds and pulled his shoes from underneath. He quickly tied them and made his way toward the center of the room, fidgeting with the small band wrapped around his wrist.

Bullett look from Guy to his own wrist. A thin band, almost like a V.I.P. pass, had already been strapped to his arm. Before he could inspect it further the entertainment center containing the tv started sliding into the wall. Guy put a hand on Bullett's chest, guiding him back a few steps as the floor split open. A thick glass box rose from the open hole in the floor, it continued to rise until the top of the glass met the surface of the ceiling and all at once the alarm and machinery both stopped. Bullett glanced from the box to Guy and back again.

"Now what?" Bullett asked half to himself.

"Step inside. It will stay here if you don't, and they have been known to hold out on dinner until their tests are done." Guy said stepping into the elevator.

"I swear, if this gets me killed I'm gonna be pissed." He squeezed into the container just barely wide enough for the two of them, still unsure as to his situation or his "roommate". Once both were fully inside, the machinery kicked up again. The glass door closed as the box lowered into the darkness below feeling more like a coffin than an elevator.

---------- Chapter 6 ----------

Having descended into the floors below, light came shining into the cramped elevator. A bright room lay before them, colossal compared to their confined room, where light flowed from somewhere within the walls rather than above them. Everything was white from ceiling to floor except for the few objects before them. The room itself was divided into two sections by a glass divider running down the middle. On one side a standard set of barbells, a free-standing rock wall, and a punching bag. On the other, a wooden chair and a single plastic table with a dozen or so bowls on top, all different colors, sitting on a rather large rotating platform.

"This is new," Guy said, moving towards a panel on the wall near the first side.

"What is all this?" Bullett stood trying to figure out exactly what he was looking at.

"How should I put it?" He unnecessarily stroked his chin. "Recess? Something like that."

Guy waved his armband in front of the panel and part of the glass slid aside forming a doorway. Bullett continued to stand in awe. Not of the room anymore but of the door itself. A solid panel of glass sliding with no wheels, wires, plastic, or metal. His eyes could perceive nothing but a solid wall of glass opening like magic. He was just as fine to ponder the physics of that for the next few hours rather than study what was in the other room. Guy urged him to find out what his room held though as the surprise would be just as fun for him.

Mimicking Guy, Bullett put his own armband next to the panel on the opposite side of the room. His door opened just the same yet, instilled a sense of amazement all over again. He stepped up to the chair and took a seat. Each bowl in front of him contained a mundane item. *Let's see… water, sand, a lighter and super tiny candle, marbles, confetti, one of those hand fan thingys, ugh, what's the point in all of this?*

He spun the platform quicker than he meant to, causing several of the containers to fly off in different directions. A few feathers stuck to the wall onto something that could be some kind of sap or honey. A cluster of pellets scattered off the table while a bowl containing various types of string (or perhaps hair) spun wildly. A metal ball bounced softly across the floor stopping on the toe of his shoe. He stared at it, part of him wanted to leave it there as it was useless. The rest of him, however, figured with enough effort it could be beaten down into some sort of sharp razor. While he wasn't too versed on prison methods, it was really small, and he wasn't much of a fighter. He knew though, if done right, it could be made into a weapon of some sort.

Guy had been exercising on the various equipment provided yet he never took an eye off of Bullett. He was intrigued by his cautious approach to everything that laid in front of him, almost as if he were solving a puzzle. He could tell tiny connections were being made in his mind, forming a bigger picture. After picking up two forty pound barbells, he eyed the rockwall for a moment before ascending to the top using only his feet. Upon reaching the top, he hooked his legs over the edge and started doing crunches. The cacophonous spray of bowls startled him from his rhythm.

"Having fun yet?" He then threw the barbells up as he dramatically flipped from the wall, landing like a successful gymnast just in time to catch each weight as though they were hollow replicas.

"No, this whole thing makes no sense. I mean, what's with all the random junk?" Bullett asked, gesturing to the mess before him. In a moment of clarity he remembered the pellets. Perhaps if he were quick enough he would be able to grab a few without being noticed. Though, where the cameras were hidden would be impossible to tell, but the only way to find out was to try.

"Man there's stuff everywhere! What am I even supposed to do with all this?" Bullett tried to sound genuinely upset; it helped that the past few days had been nothing but frustration.

"Better clean it up. We don't want the parents getting angry about our messes." Guy dropped the weights onto the rack with enough force to rattle the divider between them.

"Yeah I guess…" Though sounding dismayed he was mentally prepared for this moment. He first wiped all of the loose string into a bowl and placed it aside. He then moved to a random spot of the sticky sap-like goo. He wiped a bit "off" the table successfully smearing a patch on the palm of his hand. He bent down towards his shoe. *I have to be quick.*

The glass walls rattled slightly followed by the entire room lurching as if an earthquake had struck. Everything flew forward including the table and the chair he was sitting in. Bullett was thrown face first onto the floor while guy jumped over the falling equipment.

"What was that?" Bullett yelled, muffled under the table.

"I'm not sure, it happens randomly. This is maybe the third or fourth time this week." Guy said as he headed to the panel inside the room to let himself out.

Bullett wiped his face of the dirt and feathers he found himself in, successfully smearing the sticky sap on his face. "Could this be any worse?" He crawled out from under the table knocking what was left on top to the floor.

Guy walked passed his "door" towards the other panel. He swiped his band across it allowing the other door to open. "Yeah, sometimes there's an aftershock."

The ground moved again throwing Bullett through the door, Guy caught him by the arm this time holding him steady until the tremors passed. "Usually right after the quakes are over they end recess." A loud ring came over some sort of speaker system hidden from view.

Guy just pointed towards the ringing as he headed towards the elevator. "W..what happens next?" Bullett said, still shaken from the previous quakes.

Guy stepped into the box. "Time for bed." He smiled and held the elevator door as if at a hotel. Bullett stepped in as the lights turned off in the room leaving them in a pitch black enclosed space. Bullett, already way out of his comfort zone, pressed his back to one of the walls.

Guy leaned over and whispered. "You know roughly 13 people die every year by vending machines?" Both rode in silence the rest of the way up. Their minds wandering from one place to the other; memories of home, ways to escape, the oddity of their new "roommate" and who or what was keeping them there all held a brief train of thought.

Arriving back in their room, the scenery had changed slightly. The alarm clock and smoke detector were both gone. Guy was the first to notice commenting on how "they" were listening so he didn't harp on it for long. Bullett went to the bathroom to clean up.

The bathroom itself was more of the basics of a bathroom without actually being one. One tiny sink with a rectangular piece of reflective faux metal to serve as a mirror, a toilet without a lid, and a drainage pipe in the floor with a hose to serve as the shower. The room as a whole stood out from the rest of what he'd seen so far. This room felt more like prison than any other.

Guy turned on the tv, while it was only one channel and all infomercials at night, he normally tried to catch the news. He found it hard to believe anyone would make weeks worth of fake news with video to compliment it. And if it was all old news stories, eventually, some information would slip that they hadn't caught. One way or another this was his one connection to the outside world right now.

Bullett cupped the lukewarm water in his hands allowing water to overflow. The sink only had an on and off rotating handle, not allowing for temperature adjustment. He scrubbed with the provided off-brand soap, getting the sticky substance off his hands before working up a lather for his face. He glanced up at the makeshift mirror and paused. He didn't recognize himself.

Is that me… I look like death. When was the last time I slept? His thoughts roamed to the past days he could remember. He'd almost died twice but that seemed like a dream now. He pulled up his pant leg. *No scars? I should have severe scar tissue from that.* He took off his shirt and examined his body in the mirror. *No stab wounds or marks, and now that I look I have a lot more muscle definition.* He flexed his arms, to his surprise his normal flabby arms responded with a pump of muscle reminding him of Popeye after his spinach. *This isn't real, none of this makes sense. Not only should I be torn and barely alive, but I look like I've been working out. Holy crap! I have a 4-pack… not quite a 6-pack but I'm getting there!* He quickly dried his face with a scratchy towel and threw his shirt back on, heading back to show his roommate.

"… thick fog swallowing everything for the third day in a row. Police are urging people to drive slowly and be extra careful in high population areas. Back to you Brian." The weather report wrapped up and some story about a new gun law droned on. Guy glanced over to Bullett walking in.

"Your shirt's on backwards." He said as he turned to untuck the covers from the bed.

Bullett ignored his comment. "So hey… are you… like... different from before you were here?"

Guy stopped and sat down on the bed. Turning with a glimmer of humor in his eyes. "Awww do I need to teach the little Jackrabbit about the birds and the bees?"

"What? No! Nothing like that, I'm saying I look like I worked out for the past month. I mean I'm not *ripped* but I've put on muscle and it doesn't make sense."

"Well now that you mention it, I have noticed I'm quite a bit more fit than I was before. But my muscle structure is about the same. I mean, I did practice martial arts so I probably had a bit more tone than you did so I haven't felt a huge difference."

"It just doesn't feel right, like something is different and I have no idea what." Bullett sat on his bed sighing and turning his shirt around.

Guy glanced back at the tv his eyes going wide. "Did you just see that?!" Bullett had just pulled his shirt back over his head.

"See what?" He followed Guy's gaze to the tv. Some story about a traffic accident played out, something like twenty three cars in a pile-up. Some force of nature causing gasses to erupt under a section of road causing several cars to flip and others to slam into each other. They looped several scenes including a dash-cam from a cop car.

"There!" Guy said jumping to his feet pointing to a corner of the screen. "The guy in the back, watch him!"

The scene started over from a nearby building's surveillance camera. Bullett watched carefully at the man Guy was still pointing at. He stood near the back of a crowd by the street. The man wore a jacket, sunglasses and a baseball cap all of which help make it difficult to identify him. He appeared to be waiting at a crosswalk at an intersection of two busy roads. For the first few seconds he did nothing but stand; after several seconds he took one of his hands out of his pocket and lifted it as though holding a basketball. Simultaneously the earth in front of him rose and split with enough force to throw cars and cause the massive pile-up.

Both men stared at the tv, even as the news changed to something else neither broke their fixated eyes from the spot he once stood. After several minutes Guy turned to Bullett. "You saw that right?" Bullett could only nod, still staring at the tv. *What the hell is happening?* The lights dimmed in the room throwing Guy back into routine and Bullett back in confusion.

"Time for bed." Guy said already rolling into his pillows and pulling up the blankets.

"I take it if you don't sleep something bad happens?" Bullett said already pulling up his own covers.

"They *do* like their schedules." Guy recited as if he'd already answered this question.

"I don't know if I'll be able to sleep, my mind is racing." Bullett stared at the ceiling. He imagined eyes staring back at him and couldn't help but imagine death standing above him just waiting for him to close his eyes. For some reason it was comforting, he'd been so close to death that his embrace would be welcome.

"Oh, just out of curiosity why do they call you Bullett?" Guy said glancing back. Bullett snored softly. Guy shrugged and rolled to face the wall. *A story for another time perhaps.*

---------- Chapter 7 ----------

An alarm buzzed throughout the room loud enough to wake the dead. Guy jumped to his feet and headed to the small desk which already had two trays of food and a change of clothes for each of them. Bullett had rolled over in his sleep, leaving him balanced on the edge of the bed. The alarm blaring from the ceiling startled him just enough to put him face first on the floor with his legs wrapped in the blanket.

After he freed himself from his sleep-cocoon he made his way towards the smell of food. Though it smelled good the looks of it left a lot to be desired. Everything was textbook cafeteria food from the way too dry toast to the overly soggy eggs. Though after he took his first bite of microwaved bacon he realized just how hungry he really was, his groggy demeanor melted as his stomach filled. He scarfed down his meal and downed the orange juice as quickly as he could then placed his tray and drink on top of Guy's, already finished and back on the desk.

"Get dressed princess. They started testing me from day one, so I'm gonna go ahead and assume they'll do the same to you."

64

Guy reached to turn on the tv only to realize it was missing. "Dammit, now how am I supposed to watch my soaps?" He glanced over to Bullett. "How are you at shadow puppets?" Bullett just stared at him blankly, then went back to tying his shoe.

Once both were dressed the elevator rose through the floor as before. Bullett watched as brick and steel passed by on the other side of the glass wondering what "tests" waited for him and what the true intentions behind all of this was.

The elevator slowed as it stopped at a room covered in cloth. Everything in the room was off-white, except for one very thin black line stretched from wall to wall. The walls, ceiling and floor all looked like they had a canvas coating stretching into tiny slits in the walls themselves. All except for the area behind them, it was solid brick with some thick plastic coating on the wall. The room ran almost 50 yards long yet was only as wide as their bedroom. A gentle hum surrounded them.

Bullett was the first to step out onto the floor. The cloth dipped slightly onto a hard surface underneath. It felt like a trampoline over concrete. "It's a little springy." Bullett said, looking over to Guy who seemed to be inspecting the ceiling like a piece of art.

Guy just nodded while staring intently at the corners and crevices in the room, he smiled almost to himself and stepped out of the elevator. The door closed and it rose back into the ceiling.

"What is this room?" Bullett asked, looking to Guy for guidance.

"Not sure, it's a different test every time." Guy snapped to the wall behind them. "Something's happening though."

Bullett turned around, the plastic wall now had holes the size of baseballs dotting it. Sharp metal spikes slowly revealed themselves from inside extending several feet from the wall. Both men looked to each other in confusion, Guy had a sudden realization and couldn't help but smirk.

"Things are about to get interesting." Guy said as he turned, walking towards the other end of the room. Echoes of machinery sounded throughout the room leaving a reverberating quake in their bones. The floor rocked slightly like a train coming to a stop. Bullett was pulled closer to the protrusions staring him in the eye. He took a step backwards almost tripping, still not used to the new footing.

"What's going on?" He said turning towards Guy who was already halfway to the other side of the room. Bullett jogged to catch up, the floor jerked again harder this time. Both barely stayed on their feet. A chugging sound bellowed from beneath them and the floor pulled again but this time it didn't stop. The entire room became one big treadmill pushing them both towards the certain death sticking from the bricks behind them.

"Hurry!" Guy called over his shoulder, unable to hide the fear he felt. None of the other tests had been life-threatening before this one and so Guy never felt anything more than amusement at the tests he'd taken. Today, however, the sickening realization washed over him. *These aren't just simple tests, these are experiments... and the rats are expendable.*

Bullett jogged to catch up, though his pace wasn't to par. As he moved the floor picked up pace, keeping him only yards from a certain painful death. Guy slowed just enough to stay slightly ahead of Bullett. "Listen man," Guy said. "this isn't the same as everything else. We *will* die if we don't finish it. If I've learned anything so far, it's that the tests don't end till they're over."

Bullett felt his heart drop into his stomach; the adrenalin-fueled terror he'd thought behind him returned with a vengeance. He wasn't a runner, he avoided physical activity if at all possible. His mind was in shambles.

This can't be happening, they wouldn't actually let us die would they? I can't die like this, at least I'm not alone. Is he gonna die before me? No. No, he's more physically fit. But, he isn't leaving me behind. Maybe I can hold out,

I mean… I've been through worse just this week. That's right! I should be dead already, multiple times! I can do this, whatever this is I'll claw my way through it if I have to. I'm not about to go out here, not like this.

Invigorated, Bullett leaned forward into a run. He ran beside Guy trying to remember everything he knew about running. *Breathe in through the nose and out through the mouth. Or was it the other way around? Ugh, skip that. Elbows bent, center of gravity forward allowing my body to push up and off the ground, line up my knees and feet and finally relax… yeah right.*

Though he lacked confidence Bullett pressed forward, inching his way towards the front of the room. Guy paced himself to Bullett staying side by side with him. Bullett glanced toward the floor in front of him and quickly noticed the black line heading back their direction. He and Guy turned to look at each other simultaneously, both realizing they had made it back to the starting point. Guy crossed the line first. The room began shaking again as the walls and floor seemed to bubble. Large square blocks formed underneath the canvas just ahead of them, stationary under the moving cloth.

The blocks grew disproportionate, the one in front of Guy being larger, finally stopping their growth somewhere between knee and naval height. Almost as if liquid, one of the blocks moved with the speed of the rotating room. Bullett had to jump out of the way, almost tripping on his own feet, avoiding it. He regained his stride noticing he was behind Guy now.

"Jump!" Guy called as the second block approached. He cleared it like an Olympic runner. Bullett, slower to react, barely managed to hop over the obstacle. Struggling to stay vertical, he fell further behind Guy who, by this point, was pulling ahead of the midway point.

Slowly regaining stride Bullett started pulling away from the metal spears behind him. Working his way forward, he watched as the black line passed underneath him again. Ahead of them both walls had pillars extending towards each other meeting in the center of the room. The blockade paused just long enough for them to decide if going over or under would be safer.

Guy took the high road and jumped, planting a single hand on it letting both legs fly to the side, clearing it with ease. Bullett decided on sliding under it as if making it to first base, unfortunately for him the material making up the floor created more friction than dirt or grass. He slid just long enough for a large section of his pants to be ripped away exposing most of his leg.

Both men, however, made it past the obstacle and continued their run. Guy kept his pace allowing for Bullet to catch up. By the time the line passed again they were both prepared. A horizontal beam on one side and a vertical one from the ceiling formed a square space, dividing the two as they dodged. A second wave of obstacles came before the line passed this time. They were growing accustomed to this trial.

Again, the starting line passed them, this time though, several dozen small blocks formed on all surfaces. Each had to hop and spin to prevent from tripping. Guy jumped onto the wall, running for several seconds before jumping into a spin landing just beside Bullett. Neither had said a word to each other in a while, almost as if they didn't need to. The rules were clear, last one dead wins.

Minutes ticked by, impossible to track, the two were moving in a dead sprint though they couldn't quite tell how fast they were moving in a blank room. Slowly the entire room had become misshapen and jagged, neither touched the ground for more than a moment as they hopped along flat surfaces. Guy kept to the walls and ceiling as Bullet trekked a path along the floor, both certain they wouldn't lose to the other.

With little warning all movement stopped causing them to dash forward through the room. Guy managed to land feet first against the wall and drop gracefully to the ground. Bullett slammed into the wall with an echoing thud. He collapsed to the ground breathing heavily. "Is that it? Did we win?" He choked out between breaths.

"I don't know." Guy said, doubled over watching his sweat drip. "That was… intense."

A buzzer sounded and the spikes receded. The elevator descended from the ceiling once more. With their only reward being life, both hobbled over to the elevator. Their game ending in a lie.

Dinner and a fresh change of clothes awaited them in their room. Bullett decided on a shower before indulging in either. The water temperature was lukewarm at best and smelled of chemicals. *Are they brainwashing us with the water?* He shrugged it off, he was better off being a zombie unless he could find a way out of there.

He dressed and switched out with Guy. After both showered and ate, the buzzer sounded for lights out. "It hasn't been that long already has it?" Bullett asked Guy as he untucked his blanket.

"I already told you, in this place even time is an illusion." Guy said adjusting his pillow.

"Get what sleep you can while you can. They could wake us up in ten minutes or ten hours, there's no telling."

Night passed for Bullett like vapor; his bones ached, his muscles hurt, and his mind raced. Some hours later he heard a noise across the room like a hydraulic pump. He looked across his blanket towards the source. Just above the writing desk the wall had slid open revealing a small rectangular opening. In the dim light he could just barely make out two figures on the other side. They stood in a hallway just beyond their room. Both wore uniforms befitting battle with semi-automatic weapons slung over their backs. *Marines? Maybe special ops.* They placed clothes and food on the desk. Once both were done placing their items the wall section slid back into place with a hiss, locking into place.

Moments later the alarm sounded. Guy rolled out of bed and walked towards the food looking as though he'd had a full night's rest. Bullett stumbled over and grabbed his tray.

The air was heavy, both dreading the next testing round. Guy was the first to break the silence. "Did you know three in five adults have a classifiable mental disease?" Bullett looked up from his food.

"Classifiable meaning *any* condition? Makes sense, there's so many diseases out there that pretty much anyone would fall into one or another." Guy nodded. Neither were physically or mentally prepared for what was to come and they both knew it.

Bullett's appetite diminished the longer he thought about their situation. He put his tray on the bed beside him. Forehead resting on the palms of his hands, he stared at his shoes trying to will them onto his feet. The soles were worn already from the previous test. The interweaving pattern on the tread was worn to almost nothing at the front yet the heel remained as if it were never walked on.

A glimmer in the heel of one of the shoes stopped him. Gingerly picking up the shoe he looked in between the treads for that glimmer again. Sunk deep into the rubber, a pellet stared back igniting a spark of hope. He stared, fixated on how to get it out as it was too deep for his fingernails to grasp.

"What are you doing?" Guy asked, setting down his tray.

"Just looking at how worn these are." He tossed the shoe to Guy.

Guy inspected the shoe, uninterested and still in thought himself. Bullett watched him, hoping, maybe even praying he would see this small chance at *something*. His eyes twitched for just a moment. *Did he see it?* He flipped the shoe over a few times, inspecting all angles. Apathetic, he handed the shoe back.

"I stick with good ol' fashioned Chucks myself." He picked up his own shoe. "The inside of these is what really makes them worthwhile. How about yours?" He arched an eyebrow.

"Meh, they're alright I guess." Bullett said, glancing at his own shoe. "I don't really pay that much attention honestly."

Guy slapped his own forehead. "God, I know... you are the worst at paying attention."

The alarm blared stopping them both. They scarfed down a few more bites of food and quickly dressed. The floor split open as two elevators rose. One covered in bars like a cage. They glanced at each other, one was going to have to be in the cage.

"Take your pick. You've been here longer." Bullett said slipping on a shoe.

"I'll take the normal one, I promised an old friend my cage dancing days were over."

Bullett stood, stepping into his other shoe. A pain shot through him. His foot felt as though hot coals were burning into his skin. He kicked the shoe off and tore off his sock. Guy just watched in confusion. Bullett scanned the skin on his foot for injuries. There was nothing. Not a mark nor blemish save for a small silver speck by his toe. On cue it burrowed into the skin leaving no trace of ever being there.

He just stared at his foot blankly. He scratched and rubbed where it once was but nothing felt out of place. Guy put a hand on his shoulder. "Umm you ok there?" Bullett figured he was dreaming and yet, he felt as though something truly significant happened. He put his shoe back on and stepped into the caged elevator.

This one was slightly different from the other. It was double layered with some sort of metal bars in-between the layers of glass. Everything was barred, from the sliding door in front of him, to the ceiling and floor. The ominous sound of the door locking into place made him uneasy. "See you on the other side." Guy said as he stepped into his own box, both slowly descended into the darkness below.

Bullett stared at his feet until the shaft closed above him enveloping him in shadow. Moments of echoing passed as he traveled further below. With no warning his ride came to a jerking halt. Mechanical shifting and buzzing surrounded him for a few seconds before everything became deathly silent. He could hear his own heart beating and his breath seemed to echo in whatever room he was in. "You there?" Guy called, causing Bullett to nearly jump out of his skin.

"Uh y..yeah." Bullett reached out to the glass in front of him only to find it had been removed, leaving only the bars behind.

His hand brushed past a bar and he felt it. An indescribable moment coursed through him. At first he couldn't make sense of it; an abstract jumble of information hitting his brain. The metalic taste of blood.

Then, slowly, gracefully, it became a picture. In a complete moment of clarity he could *feel* the metal, as if it were part of him. Where it connected, it's nicks and faults, where it was most sturdy and even how dense it was, all formed a mental picture the likes of which he'd never experienced.

He dropped to the floor, his head spun and his blood ran hot. *What WAS that?* He put a hand beneath him to push up. His palm, landing firmly on another bar, sent more waves of information to him. Struggling to make sense of it he sat motionless, hand underneath him in a half crouch for what seemed like hours. His brain felt as though someone poured pop-rocks on it.

One of the vertical bars to his side vibrated slightly, pressure was being applied to the middle across a few inches. "I see," Guy said standing on the other side. "So you're in a cage. I don't like this." Above them a large scraping sound cut through the silence, the echoing making it twice as loud. Bullett, still sat in a daze, his mind bombarded with a sixth sense he couldn't make heads or tails of.

"What is that?" Guy yelled over the sound. He reached passed the bars, groping in the darkness until he grabbed a fist full of Bullett's shirt. "Hey man, you ok?" He yelled shaking him.

Bullett, still shaken, somewhat came to his senses. "Y..yeah!" He yelled over the, now thunderous noise. Guy pulled on his shirt lifting him off the ground.

The metal faded from his mind, leaving an emptiness inside him. It felt as though he had lost an arm and couldn't remember when or how. Above them something thudded on top of the bars causing the scraping to stop. A light dimly lit up against a wall far across the room revealed two things. One, they were in a large rectangular room completely barren save for a small torch on the wall. And two, there was a large stone block taking up about half of the room being held up solely by the bars Bullett was contained in.

Guy was the first to react, throwing both hands up to help push the block up. Bullett followed suit and also pressed both hands against the stone. For such a large object it didn't take much effort for the two to lift it. It raised several inches from the cage, as it did the torch across the room burned brighter. Guy turned to Bullett. "We gotta get you out of there!" His face was draped in shadow yet his fear could clearly be seen. Bullett nodded staring ahead, almost unaware of the danger he was in.

Something shimmering in the light caught his attention on the wall opposite of them. "What's that?" Bullett said nodding towards it. Guy squinted. "Hard to tell from here. This thing is pretty light though, can you hold it for a sec?" Bullett just nodded again, his attention on the bars above him.

Guy dropped his arms and sprinted to the other side of the room. A small silver keypad imbedded into the wall awaited him with a digital interface reading "3 attempts left". Above it words had been written on the wall by some sort of marker or pen.

"So this doesn't look good. It's some kind of puzzle." Guy said over his shoulder.

Bullett didn't react. He stood with one hand on the block, the other on one of the bars above him. He closed his eyes, he could still clearly see his entrapment in his mind's eye. *How… is this possible? What exactly are these made of?* He opened his eyes again, Guy was shouting something to him.

"Hey! Heyyyy! Are you ok man?" Guy ran back over to help lift again. "Did this get heavier?" Bullett shrugged. "What's with you Bullett? You sick or something?" He contemplated his answer.

"Touch the bars." Bullett said dryly.

"What? I don't know if you quite understand what's happening but I'm pretty sure we're on a timer." The block above them shook slightly, it's weight seemed to double. Bullett remained lucid enough to release his grip on the metal poles and push back against the weight.

The two just stared at each other in silence for a moment. Bullett's eyes pleaded with Guy who gave up trying to find logic in the moment. "Oh fine!" He brought down a hand and slapped the bars. "Happy?" He said pushing back up.

"Did you feel anything?" Bullett asked, almost begging.

"Feel what? I felt a metal pole. I also feel a big-ass rock about to crush you." Guy snapped back.

Defeated, Bullett resigned himself crazy and decided to try to ignore this despite his curiosity."Well then, what now?" He asked Guy as though he just walked in on the situation.

"What now? What n.. where have you been?! There's the ceiling dropping on top of you, a keypad, a note, and apparently I've been alone up until now. Welcome to the party!"

"Ah.." Bullett said matter of factly. "..so it's like one of those puzzle games where you're on a timer and locked in a room. Got it." Guy opened his mouth prepared with a plethora of insults but he was cut off. "What's the note say? Any of the keys look different? Anything on the ceiling?"

Guy bit his tongue saving his choice words for another time. "I don't know, why don't you go look for yourself..." With no warning Guy released his hold on the stone and stormed back across the room. The room got darker as Bullett struggled to hold it all on his own.

"Let's see...." Guy pretended to study the keypad with great interest. "Nope, nothing." Bullett's arms were already feeling heavy, the ceiling vibrated again then increased in weight. It slammed down on top of the bars causing it to rattle loudly. Guy started to sprint back towards him. "No!" Bullett yelled, "we're on a timer. Look for clues! You said there was a sign, what does it say?"

Guy hesitated. "Seriously if that's getting heavier you won't be able to hold it on your own for long."

"All the more reason to hurry then isn't it?" Bullett said gritting his teeth and doing all he could to hold the rock up.

"All roads. That's all it says." He looked to the ceiling, nothing there. He looked back to Bullett when something caught his eye. "Hey! There's something carved into the rock. "MILD" All capital letters."

Bullett closed his eyes. "That's everything you see, nothing else?"

"That's it." Guy said. "Wait, if you take the word mild and use an old school phone the numbers would be 6453." Bullett started to feel the burn in his legs as well. "Try it!" Another shake and the stone pounded into the bars causing them to bow in various directions. "Didn't work, says two attempts lefl!" Guy shouted.

"Alright, wait before you try again. Come help me hold this, two clues is probably all they gave us." Guy dashed back toward him, sliding under and pushing up on the stone. Bullett glanced over. "Was there anything else in the message above the keyboard? Like punctuation, capital letters, or anything misspelled?"

"Capital A and three dots at the end. Why?" Guy asked.

"Give me a sec to think." *All roads...* Bullett's mind raced. *Roads, highways, interstates, avenues... no probably not one of those. Mild? Mild roads or all roads are mild? Could it be what they're made of? No that's a bit of trivia that'd be too impossible. All roads... All roads... mild... All roads M.I.L.D.!*

"Roman numerals!" Bullett's shout took Guy by surprise. "Wh..what?" Bullett would have laughed out loud if his body wasn't nearing it's limit. The weight increased yet again, this time it crushed the bars as though they weren't there, causing both men to drop to a squatting position. They didn't have long. "All roads lead to Rome!

All the letters in mild are in the roman numeral system. I is 1, M is 1000, D is 500 but I can't remember L."

"Well make it fast cause I don't think we can survive another drop. I'm not even sure you'll make it out if I leave..." His words stung them both. One or both of them was not going to make it out of this.

"Well what are the options?" Guy said trying to sound hopeful.

"Well it could be 50 or 5000. We have two attempts so if you're fast enough we may both make this." Guy could see the sweat soaking through his clothes and the way his muscles shook. If he left he would be condemning Bullett, if he stayed it would be suicide. "1551" Bullett stated calmly. "Either that or 6501. Flip a coin on which you try first but those are pretty much our only options. If you move quick and God-willing that's the answer I'll see you on the other side, if not well... it was an honor to meet you." Guy wanted to protest but he knew he was right.

"You ready?" Guy asked, shoving up against the stone with all his strength. "Go! I have a plan." Bullett dropped to his back and used his legs as a brace, they at least had more strength left than his arms. Guy dropped low and dug his feet down as hard as his shoes allowed. He burst forward in a blur and made it across the room in a flash. Bullett grabbed a bar and pulled it, trying to use it to push up as well. Guy pounded the numbers on the keypad, he submitted his result and received the message "1 attempt remaining" He tried the other combination.

Bullett was at the end of his strength. He prayed the bars would resist long enough. The stone shook. Eyes wide he could do nothing but yell. Guy hit enter and turned in time to see the stone drop to meet the floor silencing Bullett's scream. His eyes watered, a sickening feeling washing over him. The lamp on the wall above him hissed and went dark. He felt the floor give way beneath him as he fell into darkness.

---------- Chapter 8 ----------

The dark control room lit up as light poured in from the open door, almost blinding the operator who sat behind the series of monitors. Startled, he shielded his eyes as a man entered and let the door close behind him. "What did you do that for? You could at least knock and warn somebody first." said the operator.

"Sorry for the headache, but I've come to see how my new friends are doing." The man's voice was flat but seemed friendly enough. Or at least about as friendly as you get in a place like this. He leaned over the operator's shoulder and glanced between the monitors.

"I'm sure you know you can't be in here without a proper ID scan." The operator said as he held out his hand, waiting for the man's badge.

"Of course. My name is Leon." He reached for and shook the operator's outstretched hand and reached into his jacket with his other hand. Leon pulled out a black leather billfold and placed it in the operator's hand in exchange for his own.

"Gabriel," the operator said opening the billfold. "What is this?" Gabriel took the plastic card from its sleeve and turned it over several times. "There is no information on this card. It's just your picture and the word "Leon". No rank or title or department. You could have made this at home."

A half smile creeped onto Leon's face and he chuckled slightly. "That's very funny. I suppose you could, though it wouldn't open nearly as many doors." He motioned for Gabriel to scan his card.

Gabriel slid the ID through the computer's reader and was visibly taken aback by what he saw. "My apologies sir. I … I had no idea. I've never seen a security clearance this high, though, it still doesn't say what department you're from. Of course you'll have access to whatever information you need."

""Sir" isn't necessary Gabriel. Just Leon. We're both grown men here, no need for shiny pleasantries. Like these trials and this facility, I am only a rumor you may or may not have heard of. Now show me the reports and pull all video footage linked to room 57 regarding their first two trials. I like to start from the beginning."

The operator had the monitors spring to life with a few swift keystrokes. In seconds he had two monitors showing trial footage on loop, while a few others pulled up several series of documents on the two inhabitants of room 57. "This is everything we have on them", Gabriel narrated, " complete with detailed background histories and physical changes updated by the hour. As with the other specimens, both show an increase in strength and agility, as well as an increase in cell repair and regeneration. The first to arrive, one Guy, Francis age 24, appears to have an increase in agility well above that of the others we've seen but does not appear to exhibit any additional defensive reactions as of yet."

Leon continued to stare at the two trial videos, almost as if he was watching both at once. Gabriel paused to try and judge a reaction, but after a few moments of silence, continued with his evaluation. "The second to arrive, one Jones, Luke age 26, has yet to exhibit any noticeable defensive reactions at all."

"Interesting indeed. It seems to me they haven't had enough stimulus. They need to be put in danger." Leon kept the smirk as he made his suggestion.

Gabriel pulled up and highlighted the description and results of the second trial. "I would think they were in plenty of danger during trial 174. Jones was almost impaled when he tripped here." He pointed out the scene on the footage.

Leon leaned over and slammed his fist down on the keyboard, prompting an error message to appear on a few of the screens. "Clearly it wasn't enough was it? They have already started relying on each other. They want to be a team? Great! We will test that teamwork.

Put them in 313!" Leon stood back up and straightened the cuffs on his sleeves. His calm smile returned. "I expect a full report and bioanalysis on my desk before noon tomorrow."

The operator nervously tried to get his keyboard to work again. 'Absolutely sir. Of course." A thought suddenly struck him, "Where is your office?" The door closed before he could finish his sentence.

About the time Gabriel's eyes adjusted to the darkness of the control room again, another of his coworkers burst through the door. "Is it true? Is Leon himself here to oversee the experiments?"

"Oh yes, and what a fun guy he is Bandera." Gabriel said while covering his eyes. "He looked over the reports of room 57 and then flipped out, yelling about how we need to REALLY test them. Then he told me to schedule test 313. I don't even know who is in charge of scheduling tests! On top of all that he wants a full report on his desk tomorrow. I didn't even know he had on office!"

Agent Bandera laughed. "Thats Leon. I've heard people talking about him. Anywhere he is at the time is his office and any surface he is close to is his desk, and he is arrogant enough to expect someone to run around the entire facility to find him to hand him a piece of paper. All that said, people say he is the most brilliant mind the government has to offer. I even heard he has singlehandedly overthrown a dozen of the world's top political figures just to have ones "more suitable" to him take power."

Within the hour the next test was set up and they delivered food and a change of clothes to room 57's residents. Leon walked back into the control room just as the elevators began rising into the room. He called to someone who appeared to be his assistant, and gave instructions before pulling up a chair beside Gabriel. Gabriel proceeded to go over the details of the trial they were about to see.

"As you know, the purpose of this trial is to test how well the two work together and solve problems in a highly stressful situation. One subject will be placed in the cage while the other is free to move about the testing area. The only source of light available to them is a gas-powered torch set behind the stone block that is atop elevators."

They watched as the elevators lowered into the testing area. Leon's assistant walked back into the control room and handed his superior a large bucket of popcorn, which Leon took with a smile.

"Popcorn sir?" Gabriel asked, more than a little confused.

"What's a movie without popcorn? You kids don't know how to appreciate the small things anymore." Leon replied with a mouth half-full of his snack.

Gabriel continued with his explanation as they watched their two subjects scramble around their latest trial. "The stone is fitted on a counterweight system. Every sixty seconds a weight is removed from the opposite side. When weight is removed, the stone will become heavier. It continues in this manner until the cage can no longer support the weight and both are crushed."

"Shhh. You're talking through the movie." Leon was smiling as he watched the two pawns navigate his chessboard. The first code was entered and the monitor flashed with the failed attempt. The stone dropped lower, bending the bars of the cage. The men on the screen became frantic, talking through every possible answer before entering anything else into keypad. "Only two tries left little mice."

Gabriel nervously glanced over at Leon. "If you don't mind me asking sir, what exactly are we trying to do here?"

"Something extraordinary has happened. Due to a happy accident with our logistics division we have been handed an opportunity to push the boundaries on a global stage." Leon replied without looking from the screen.

"So we are training them to be soldiers?"

"No, no. We don't need more soldiers. We need something better. We have a chance to eliminate the need for war all together. When you control the monster, what is there left to fear?"

The stone dropped once again, causing the one in the cage to drop into a crouch. Leon listened as they started deciphering the puzzle and ran to try another code. "Code Successful" blinked in front of him. Gabriel reached for the button to stop the test. "Wait!" Leon yelled, "Let them sweat."

Gabriel couldn't help himself. "Another minute and these men will be dead and we will lose two more subjects!"

"Fine, fine. You really take the sport out of this." Leon quipped as the button was pressed and the floor of the testing area fell away.

"Well … they survived." Gabriel said, trying to ignore Leon's last comment. "What now sir?"

"Give them a day's rest. Then schedule them for test 11. Use the subjects from room 23."

"Test 11? Sir with all due respect, that test was scheduled weeks from now. We still need a lot of data before we can …"

"They survived didn't they?" Leon interrupted as he walked from the room.

---------- Chapter 9 ----------

Guy rolled to his side gasping for breath. It felt as though he had been under water near drowning and he was taking the breath to save his life. He opened his eyes and saw a familiar wall. He was in his bed, he stared at the little scratches in the paint from when he tried to claw his way out. Turns out they didn't use drywall, instead some sort of hardened synthetic material. His head pulsed and his muscles burned. The last thing he could recall was falling into the darkness then struggling for breath... and Bullett.

Guy curled into a fetal position. He knew this place was dangerous but he never truly thought they'd let someone die. Somewhere deep in the recesses of his mind he was counting on the fact that they were too special to be expendable. His heart hurt. He pressed a hand to his chest and slowed his breathing. It pulsed normally, if he concentrated he could feel the blood passing through it. As far as he could tell it was fine, which meant he felt a genuine emotion... he hated those.

Guy traced a finger around the missing paint. He had no motivation, no energy to put into today. Though they had only been together for a few days he had forged a friendship from his partner in captivity. Guy maneuvered onto his back subconsciously avoiding making eye contact with the other side of the room. The ceiling stared back at him. It felt closer now than ever before. The room was the same size, he knew that, he had memorized its every length and angle. And yet, everything felt encased. Like somehow he was on display.

A strident noise caught him off guard. There were three times in Guy's life that he was ever really caught by total surprise. Once when he was 11 and had a surprise birthday party at Six Flags, another when he was 13 and met his favorite hockey player, and finally when he was 20 a snake found it's way to the driver's seat of his car. Guy is now the proud owner of a Ball Python named Wesley. This, however, took top spot for the biggest shock he'd ever experienced. Laying on the other bed Bullett gasped for breath, sitting fully upright and pale as a ghost.

"What the literal FUCK!" Guy shouted, simultaneously jumping from his bed. He stopped next to the bed, unsure as to hug him or punch him in the throat. Bullett's breathing slowly returned to normal. "No, like seriously man. How... what happened?"

Bullett slowly looked around the room and sighed heavily. Smiling he turned to Guy. "You did it."

Guy took a step back. "Did what?"

Bullett flopped onto his back laughing. "I was dead, I swear to God I thought I was dead. The rock was too heavy and I couldn't hold on much longer. Then at the last second the floor dropped from under me, I fell into a dark room on a pile of like mattresses or something and then the room filled with gas. You did it man, I was totally useless and you freakin' saved my life!"

Guy scratched his head. "We never would have made it out if you hadn't figured out the code. But yeah, I was pretty awesome wasn't I?"

Bullett nodded. "I owe you one." The lights went out in their room, both men sat in silence waiting for an alarm or something. The sound of a door opening drew their attention towards their door which hadn't been used since they both entered.

With a blinding brilliance the lights flashed back on, slowly dimming to their normal level. In front of them, a man dressed in an obviously expensive suit tailored to his every angle, stood adjusting his cufflinks. His tie alone looked as though it cost more than Guy's car. His shoes, however, were way out of place. Black leather Chucks adorned with scuff marks and something that appeared to be either spilled coffee or a blood stain on the toe, dramatically contrasted his otherwise absurdly expensive attire.

"Good evening gentlemen of room 57. I think we need to have a talk." The man said scanning the room.

"Oh awesome! I've been waiting all day to speak with Captain Tailor-Made. What can we do for you?" Guy replied snarkily.

"I have been watching the two of you with a great amount of curiosity. I wanted to tell you in person how glad I am that you have performed at or above our fifty percentile on all tests thus far."

"And who exactly are you? And why should we give a shit?" Guy replied.

"I am Leon. I suppose you could say I'm in charge of this facility." Leon paused for a moment. "Your friend doesn't seem to speak much."

"That's because he doesn't like you. I, on the other hand, am a huge fan so far."

Bullett smiled, half because he really didn't like Leon and half was credited to Guy actually knowing that without him saying anything. "Well you need not worry then Mr. Jones. After today you probably won't see me again. I try not to surround myself with mediocrity."

Guy stepped between the two. "Right, because only the most extraordinary of people come down to meet the lowly lab rats. Face it Lionell, you're just as worthless as we are."

Leon took a deep breath. "It's Leon. I was merely trying to extend an olive branch. Your next trials will be a bit more … challenging. Know I will be following your progress, or lack there of, very closely."

"Hmm. Well I tell you what Lester, you get in touch with the guys over at R&D and see if they can come up with something to test the amount of fucks I give, and I'll be happy to try it out." Guy said smiling. He could see Leon visibly redden. "If you want to really test us, give us a test that isn't only designed to kill us. And while you're at it, tell the guys upstairs that the next time they send a prissy-ass lacky into my room, I might lose my calm."

 Leon tried his best to conceal his anger but it was obvious Guy had won the exchange. Bullett grinned as Leon stormed towards the door. "Lights!" He yelled, he stood staring at the bulbs, his fury growing by the second. "I said lights dammit!" The lights dimmed and turned to complete darkness, the door slammed. As the lights flickered back on they both laughed. For the first time since both had been dragged into this hell they both laughed a heartfelt laugh. A silver lining in the abyss if there ever was one.

With a heavy sigh Bullett turned to Guy. "So, you really think we'll get out of here."

Guy wiped a tear away from his eye. "I don't think they can stop us."

Hours passed without any tests being done. They both took it as a sign of an early day. Bullett decided to take a shower before bed, he wanted to be clean and well rested for these "trials" ahead. Guy opted to do some minor cardio to keep his physique up.

Bullett stepped into the bathroom and disrobed. Looking in the mirror he was surprised by his own face. He almost didn't recognize himself. Nothing looked different and yet he knew he wasn't the same person. There was something in his eye that wasn't quite the same as it was a few weeks ago.

Stepping away, he turned to what passed as a shower, he turned the knob allowing it to gurgle up water. He tested the water a few times determining the temperature range to be from lukewarm to slightly warm. He chose the latter. A small hotel style bottle of shampoo sat in the corner, he lathered and rinsed without repeating. At some point he had sat down staring at the drain as the water poured through his hair.

He watched as the droplets left the tip of his hair and splashed off the floor as he prepared for the next day's events. The small speckles of rust indicated the shower was probably installed before the rest of their environment. The thought struck him with an idea. Slowly he placed a hand to the floor, the contours and minor defects of it as he ran his hand across the surface. He did this gently and deliberately allowing every part of his sensory system ample time to memorize the small section of floor beside him.

He closed his eyes and tried to *feel* the floor, searching for it's weaknesses and it's small irregularities. Yet, as hard as he focused, he came up empty. No vision in his head of it, no life altering reverberations… nothing. He sighed leaning his back against the wall. He played the events through his head over and over and he knew beyond a shadow of a doubt something truly significant happened and he had no idea how or why. Disheartened, he stood and turned off the shower.

Guy pounded on the door. "Hurry up man I have to pee!" Bullett, unprepared for such a loud intrusion, slipped mid-crouch landing flat on his back in the shower. "What the hell man?" He felt a catch in his leg and the sudden electric feel from before.

"Come on man you've been in there for like 30 minutes!" Guy shouted through the door.

Bullett struggled to his feet. The back of his leg provided a picture in his mind. A small circular grate. He looked down at his leg. His eyes went wide when he saw the metal drain cover stuck to his leg. He slapped it but it stuck fast. In a panic he pulled at it getting no movement from it, was as if it was part of him. "Guy! Get in here!" He yelled doing his best to find a suitable angle to reach it.

"I'm not finishing you off." Guy retorted through the door. "Just let me know when you're done, I really have to pee."

Bullett pulled at the grate. "Seriously man you've got to see this!"

"My eyes have trouble focusing on really small things. If you don't hurry I'm peeing under the door."

"Would you get in here! I think part of the shower is stuck in my leg!"

Guy, suddenly worried, threw open the door. "Dammit man at least put a towel on!" Bullett turned sideways and Guy saw the metal protruding from his leg. "Holy shit! What did you do?"

Bullett was still pulling at the grate. His senses going crazy with each touch. "It's not in my leg, it's stuck to it. I slipped and now I can't get it off." He grabbed his towel off the divider it was laid across, folded it, and quickly wrapped it around his waist. "What do I do?" He asked as he spun in circles trying to get a better view.

"Stop moving!" Guy yelled. "I can't do anything with you spinning like that." He crouched trying to examine his leg for a wound.

Bullett planted his feet and angled his leg towards Guy. "It feels weird, like I can feel it but it doesn't hurt."

Guy inspected it, he watched as it slowly wrapped around Bullett's leg forming a small piece of armor around his calf. He tapped it hearing the metal *ting* in response. "That... is crazy!" Guy looked up at his terrified roommate. "Stop for a second, you said you could feel this right?" He tapped again.

Bullett could feel exactly where he was touching and with how much force though he couldn't feel the "normal" sensations like heat or texture. "Yes, I can feel that but not quite sure how." Guy put a finger to his lips then points to his ear indicating they could be heard.

"Is it supposed to grow like that?" Guy asked. "I mean like are you making it do that?"

Bullett caught the gist. "I..I.. uh don't know. I'm not trying to." Bullett concentrated on the metal. Picturing in his mind's eye. He knew he wanted it off of him but he also craved for an answer to this newfound sensation. He closed his eyes and imagined it moving around to his shin. Guy watched as the metal crawled around Bullett's leg to the front.

"Did you feel that?" Guy asked. Bullett nodded, he pictured it working it's way up his flesh to the palm of his hand. He could feel as it worked it's way up sliding under the towel, it was smooth as though someone was running their hand up him. He opened his eyes once he felt the weight in his palm. He stared at it, the metal itself pulsed as though it had it's own heartbeat.

"It's pretty heavy in my hand but it's almost as if it's alive." Bullett said almost to himself.

"Throbbing is the word you're looking for." Guy said, reasserting the need for discretion.

Bullett touched it with his other hand, it felt malleable. He pulled at it and was able to shape it like dough. "You see that?" He asked excitedly.

"That's a neat trick." Guy said. "You think you can do that without using your hands?"

Bullett removed a hand and turned the other upside down. It still clung to his skin. He focused and mentally shaped the metal. He tried making it into a cylindrical bar at first, then tried making it flatter into a plank, then he tried sharpening the edges.

He got excited, with something like this he'd be able to fight his way out of this place. The only problem now was how to remove it from his skin. He felt his hand get lighter and glanced over just in time to watch the dagger fall into the open drain beneath him.

Guy looked to the drain then back to Bullett. "You do that on purpose?"

He shook his head, "No, this whole thing is a new experience for me."

Guy peered down the drain, somewhere in that dark void could be the key to their escape. "This stays between us ok? When the time comes for that to happen again I'll let you know when I'm ready." He arched an eyebrow.

"A..alright, I don't know how good I'll be when you're ready."

"Just do what you can to practice in your spare time and I'll do what I can to make sure we get the opportunity."

"Ok, don't count on me to perform up to your standards."

"Good" Guy said placing an arm on his shoulder. "Now get out I have to pee." He shoved Bullett through the door and closed it behind him.

Bullett got dressed and went to bed. The barrage of new experiences had him in a constant state of exhaustion. He was asleep before Guy even left the bathroom.

Guy came out of the bathroom with a plan already in mind but the where and how were the problems. He saw Bullett was already fast asleep and decided to sleep on his plan. They could always discuss it in the morning. The maze could go on forever and as long as they had a plan when they got to the cheese they should be fine.

---------- Chapter 10 ----------

Gabriel walked into the control room noting the tests being displayed on several monitors. He sat his cup and notepad next to his empty chair and turned to a gentleman staring intently at a blank screen. "Bout time for shift change, you almost done over there?" He could never remember his name.

"Just about, room 57 had an interesting conversation last night and I'm trying to isolate some background noise." He pressed rewind and hit a few keys bringing up an equalizer.

"Probably another set wanting that one last night of debauchery before cracking." He paused. "Wait, room 57? Doesn't that have two males in it?" The other guy nodded while pressing a headphone against an ear. Gabriel shrugged. "We *are* in the age of free love and all." He sat in his chair and swiped his card, logging on to his computer. He knew he was in for a long day. Since Leon had placed himself in charge of this facility, tests had doubled and everyone was working longer shifts.

He picked up his coffee, a perfect blend of cream and sugar in a toasted coconut brew. He savored the taste, closing his eyes and mentally preparing himself for the day's work. The door swung wide, slamming into the wall with a bang, announcing Leon's entrance. Gabriel jumped, dropping his coffee and simultaneously spitting some on the screen in front of him. "Sir!" He blurted while fumbling for a napkin. "We weren't expecting you, as you can see we're changing shifts. I only just got here myself."

"Nevermind that." Leon said waving his hand dismissively towards his coffee stained shirt. "I'm looking for Gabe." He said glancing around the room. Gabriel raised his hand. "Gabriel sir?" He asked sheepishly. Rumors had been swarming of Leon firing anyone he didn't find up to his standards, he knew he had skipped a report here and there but being fired over something so small seemed childish.

Leon looked him in the eyes, a fire seemed to burn within him. "Gabe is it? Good, leave everything you don't need and come with me."

Gabriel hesitated. "Am I fired sir?" Leon looked hurt.

"Good lord no, you're the one that arranged the test I wanted yes?" Gabriel nodded. "Well," Leon continued. "the person formerly in charge of that position has suffered a severe... lack of employment. Completely unrelated, you are now promoted. Now, I need you to set up the next test."

"Right away sir." Gabriel said snapping to attention. "Just two questions. What all do I take with me, and where is my office?" Leon grabbed the back of his chair and tipped it sideways, dumping him out onto the floor. He straightened his tie and looked to Gabriel. "You still have some coffee on your shirt. Meet me on the bottom floor." He walked out leaving an air of confusion in his wake.

Hours later, Gabriel had run through the gauntlet of security checks and found a door already with his name on it. He was surprised at the contrast from his last position with there only being a single computer in his office sitting atop a pewter colored metal desk. A rather large window peered over some sort of large octangular room. He pressed his face against the glass, but the only source of light came from his office, and being underground there was little chance of sun rays revealing anything.

On the screen of his computer sat a sticky note. It simply read "57 and 23, tomorrow 1300". Gabriel sighed and sat on his overly plush chair. Upon swiping his card he found he had access to a much deeper level of command than before. The new interface was user-friendly enough that he was zipping through new confidential files in no time. After a bit of snooping, he had the list of all the tests. After reading through them, he realized none allowed for two different groups to be placed together.

A flashing light in the corner of his screen caught his attention. He clicked on it and a little Cupid-looking cherub popped up on his screen. A text bubble formed above it. "I see you are trying to schedule a test. Would you like some help? Click Yes or No." *Oh good!* He thought. *I have no idea how the last guy failed at this.* After he went through a short back-and-forth with the tiny angel he had the event locked in and counting down on a timer. All that was left to do was figure out how to remove the stain from his shirt.

The timer ticked by slowly, Gabriel woke up to a small alarm on his computer indicating the event he scheduled was minutes away. He snapped awake, wiping drool from his face, and quickly tapped at the keyboard bringing both the rooms onto his screen. He watched as the elevators rose into the rooms and all participants began to lower into the floor. The camera angles then switched to a new view automatically. This angle showed a large white room with eight walls surrounding a very large pillar. Movement outside his window caught his attention.

Outside the glass he watched as the members of 23 passed by only feet away. He suddenly realized he was seated far above this circular arena-like room, now brightly lit, and he still had no clue what the "event" was. In that moment Leon walked in holding a fold-up chair and cotton candy. "Want some?" He asked, presenting Gabriel with the bag.

"Uh, sure. Thank you sir." Gabriel said hesitantly. He grabbed a small pinch.

Leon held his pose, keeping the bag presented. " Go on now, don't be shy. Its delicious!"

Gabriel grabbed a handful this time, still not sure what was going through Leon's mind. He took a bite, managing to get the sticky candy in his nose. Leon watched stone-faced, chuckled, and turned to watch the entertainment begin.

~-~-~-~-~

Guy and Bullett both took in as much scenery as possible on their way down. Every room was different and they knew to gather as much information as they could in the quickest time possible. A white room below with thick glass surrounding the top lay beneath them. A giant pillar blocked their view of the opposite side of the room but it looked symmetrical. There were chairs sitting everywhere behind the glass like a "viewing" deck, giving it more of a stadium look than a test chamber. A few people were scattered about observing as their elevator came to a stop.

Guy was the first out, making note of the angular walls and all the observers. He followed the gazes as they glanced from the other side of the room back to the duo. "This looks like a trap." Bullett said, studying at the obelisk as he stepped out.

"That part's obvious, the real question is how do we spring it?" Guy said as he walked towards a wall, staring at one of the onlookers. The sound of rapid footsteps caught his attention. He turned, barely spotting a man mid-swing, he ducked narrowly avoiding the punch. "Woah man!" He shouted catching Bullett's attention.

"What's going on? Who's that?" Bullett asked as Guy dodged a flurry of punches.

"How the hell should I know?" Guy said amidst his bobbing and weaving. He noticed two other men running around the pillar, one of whom was a complete identical to the one attacking him. "Who are you?" Guy half yelled to his attacker.

Bullett began running towards Guy but his reflexes were too slow. With no response from the stranger, Guy had already identified him as an enemy and started a counter attack. It didn't take more than a few well placed punches to down the man. As he hit the ground he dissolved like dust in the wind, as though he were never there. Guy stared at the spot where the body once was, unsure if he fought a hologram or some other trick on the mind. He wouldn't put either passed the facility.

The two strangers came running towards Guy, as soon as they caught his eye he dropped into a defensive stance. Bullett, just now noticing the two, sprinted ahead placing himself between them and Guy. "Woah!" He yelled stretching his arms out. "What is going *on* here, what was that?" He said pointing to the spot on the floor in front of Guy.

One of the two immediately stopped grabbing the other by the wrist to hold him back. A moment of silence passed as everyone caught their breath and tried to grasp the situation. The first to speak up was the twin. "You mean to tell me you guys haven't done this before?" Bullett glanced over his shoulder, receiving a shrug from Guy who dropped his stance and walked up beside Bullett

The strangers laughed, allowing Bullett a moment to process. Both were distinctly different people. One, the twin, thin and average height with slicked back hair, while the other was short and boxy and covered in tattoos. He elbowed his friend. "Looks like we're getting fresh meat." He chuckled. The thin one winced and smiled, fixing his gaze on Bullett and Guy. Though he smiled, there was a cold emotion behind his eyes. "I'm gonna give you the short and sweet version no one gave us." He said, still unable to hide his smirk. "This...

110

game… we've been put through is all a form of training. For what, I couldn't tell you, but they are teaching you to kill via your abilities."

"Abilities?" Guy interrupted.

"Yeah, like my clone you were fighting. Everyone here has some sort of ability, first they test to figure out what you can do, then they put you through more tests to make you use it, and then they make you fight to see who's the best. If you win enough you graduate and get out. If you lose… well, they don't keep their broken toys around for long."

"Woah woah woah." Guy said. "So you're telling me I killed your clone?"

He slapped his palm to his forehead. "No, I'm saying I can keep making them. Don't either of you have something special you can do that you couldn't before you got here?"

Guy and Bullett exchanged glances, they were both thinking about the incident in the shower. Neither wanted to be the one to share that secret. Guy spoke up first. "I can whistle in three octaves… oh! And I can juggle too."

Frustrated, the twin gave up. "You know what? I'm done trying to help you. Here's pretty much all you need to know, you're useless. You're either going to be killed by one of the teams or executed when you lose enough."

He held his arms out to his sides and stepped sideways, simultaneously a carbon copy stepped in the opposite direction. Though, which one was the copy was impossible to tell. Both looked exactly the same including the clothes on his back.

The shorter man inhaled sharply and held his breath. Seconds later his muscles swelled and he grew perceptively taller. He repeated the process growing in height and muscle several times. He stood almost seven feet tall in moments and his already thick muscles inflated like balloons, stretching his skin to its limits. "Consider this a lesson." He thundered.

Bullett stood dumfounded. "H...how is that even possible?" His mind was too preoccupied by the physics of such a feat to notice when all three charged forward.

Guy didn't hesitate, he dashed passed Bullett and planted a foot as he twisted, his fist already balled and mid-swing. He struck directly in the center of the stomach of the monstrosity of a man. The large man wasn't even fazed, he grabbed Guy by the throat and threw him into the outer wall like a discarded piece of trash. His mind went white as his body held on to consciousness.

Bullett snapped to attention the moment Guy was grabbed, he kicked at the man's leg doing little to injure the man. His eyes fixed on Bullett, with a bull-like rage. He lifted a single leg and kicked Bullett square in the chest, sending him sprawling backwards sliding along the ground.

Guy brought himself to his feet. He steadied himself on the wall while he regulated his breath. A fist came into view giving him only a moment to dodge out of it's path. He was struck by a second punch in the back. He stumbled forward and turned towards his attackers. Both the clone and the original stood side by side. It was impossible to tell which was the clone and which was real. He decided it'd be best to take them both out at the same time. He dashed forward with a sweeping kick.

Bullett was already exhausted, the best he could do was to block and pray he'd stay on his feet. A wide swing of rippling muscles barely grazed his arm yet the power behind it still threw him sideways. Just as his body flew into the air the man grabbed his ankle and threw him towards the pillar in the center of the room. He bounced and skidded to a halt on his knees. He looked up just as a leg flew towards him. He ducked feeling the rush of wind ripping past him. Still in movement, the giant lost his balance, falling over himself. Bullett jumped to his feet and made distance between them.

Guy swerved and twisted, dodging the fury of blows from the clone and master. He'd push one away and strike at the other. He had already destroyed three clones, yet every time he did the man would just make another. He grabbed one by the face and slammed it into a wall watching it dissolve into nothing. As his enemy made another clone a mass of muscle collapsed around the center of the room.

Bullett rounded the opposite side and sprinted towards Guy. "Mistakes were made!" He yelled as he approached. Guy turned seeing the battered friend. A hand grabbed Guy's shoulder, with a backflip and a kick another clone was dispatched, leaving the master between them both. Guy kicked the back of his leg causing him to drop to his knees. Bullett ran towards him throwing a knee into his chest. The man doubled over to the ground.

Guy threw a well placed chop to his neck knocking him unconscious. "And thank you Sensei!" He shouted triumphantly. Bullett smiled looking at the collapsed man. "One down." He looked up, smile quickly fading as he dove sideways. Guy turned just as a shoulder pounded into him, pinning him to the wall. He struggled for a few seconds then went limp. The giant grinned, turning to Bullett as Guy slid to the ground. Bullett glanced from the monster to Guy and back. He nodded to himself and ran with footsteps like explosions right behind him.

Bullett hit the wall and turned around. His foe breathed heavily. "Nowhere to run now." His voice boomed. Bullett searched the room behind him, his mind forming a plan. "Who says I'm not trying to get you away from them so I can use my ability huh?" He tried his best to sound threatening.

The large man took a half step forward and paused. Bullett didn't hesitate he dashed forward passed him, ducking under his delayed swing. He continued sprinting past the pillar drawing him away from where Guy fell. With a quick glance around the room he smiled and returned his attention to the monster charging towards him. With his momentum already going, Bullett mentally calculated his chances of his plan working with no time to prepare.

The behemoth ran towards him like a train jumping track. Bullett mentally timed his movement. Just as he was passing the pillar the words came on their own. "Get baited bitch." Bullett called diving out of the way.

The giant had noticed the movement in his peripheral too late. Already sprinting and ready, Guy ran around the center of the column and lept at the man, soaring towards him with a knee stretched forward. At that moment the giant turned to face Guy, the knee connected, shattering his jaw and cheekbone. Guy landed like a cat, on all fours, as his opponent plummeted to the floor.

He walked over to Bullett, staring at the downed man as he started to deflate back to his normal size. "Our own Goliath." Guy said as he helped Bullett to his feet. "Don't mess with them 57 boys." As battered and bruised as they were, the two started to laugh.

.

---------- Chapter 11 ----------

Several days came and went as they worked their way
from trial to trial. Guy began to train Bullett, between
tests, as best he could without seeming too suspicious.
He taught him Noudouken Ryu the way his Sensei
taught him in hope the self control and breathing would
carry over to Bullett's control over his power. He also
knew that if they were going to get out of there they
would both need to be able to fight like it was second
nature.

"Again." Guy said, assuming a defensive stance.

"It's no use." Bullett mumbled face-down on the carpet.
"You counter everything I do. I'm not getting better."

"You are getting better, you're actually learning faster
than I did." He extended a hand, helping him up. "Plus, if
I went easy on you you'd only be good against easy
opponents."

Bullett knew he was right but Guy seemed to be getting
harder and harder to fight against. The same move
never worked twice regardless of how he chained them
together. It was as if his body memorized everything it
did and perfected it without even trying.

"Alright." Bullett prepared himself. "Again."

Guy charged in first sweeping for a leg. Bullett sidestepped and thrust a hand for his chest. Guy deftly
turned throwing his shoulder forward knocking Bullett
back, he didn't allow him the chance to recuperate as he
stepped forward and placed a hand on his forehead
pushing forward. With a slight twist and a guiding hand,
Bullett landed with a thud on his back.

"See!" He shouted in defeat. "I don't stand a chance."

"While that's true, let's try a different approach." Guy said
placing distance between them. "Remember in the third
fight with the girl that could see through skin?"

"Yeah?" Bullet tried to follow his train of thought.

"Ok well this time we spar I'll fight like she did and you
try to take me down."

"Alright..." Bullett took his stance, prepared for another
defeat while Guy did his best to mimic her wide stance.
Both palms forward he felt like a sumo wrestler. Bullett
started circle walking around him. As soon as he came
within arms reach Guy shoved him backwards using
several open-handed strikes.

Shaken, Bullett approached from the opposite side. Guy
struck out again but Bullett was ready, he grabbed Guy's

wrist and pulled as he rolled away. Guy was thrown off his feet and Bullett took the opportunity to punch at his chest while he fell. Not holding back he threw his weight into his fist. He connected, launching Guy like a child's toy across the room and into the wall. He fell upside-down, landing in a hand stand.

"See? Like that. That's what I'm talking about. You may not beat me yet but you can easily beat someone else!"

Bullett stared at his fist. Since when could he hit hard enough to toss someone around? The lights went out in their room. When it came back on both were side by side and ready. Leon stood before them for a second time.

"Clarence right?" Guy asked, unsurprised by his sudden appearance.

Leon straightened his suit. "This is graduation day. I'm here to congratulate you for making it this far."

"No, no, no... Richard?" Guy pressed. "Or Dick... yeah that seems right, you look like a Dick to me."

Leon smiled. "Now now children, the time for games are over. Today you become adults or fail and get erased from existence." He moved to be face to face with Guy. "Quite honestly I'm betting on the latter."

Guy smiled. "Well sorry to disappoint but you'll neither win nor get that kiss you so desperately want."

Leon looked to Bullett. "You'll die cursing his name and, in the end, you'll never have any of the answers you seek." He spun on his heels lifting his hands. "All of this! All the secrets and security for a purpose. And the sad truth is, your only purpose is to live long enough to die to someone better than you." He said glancing behind him while walking toward the end of the room he appeared from.

"Wait!" Guy called out, causing Leon to stop and turn back around. "What size shoes do you wear?"

Leon's face remained blank as the lights went back out and he was gone as quickly as he arrived.

"Well that's good news." Guy said walking to where Leon once stood.

"What is?" Bullett stood there, almost accustomed to the random confusion of his everyday life.

"Looks like only the best make it out of here. So all we have to do is be the best."

Bullett raised his fists and bent at the knees. "Well I think we still have a ways to go."

Guy smiled. "Only one way to find out." He charged ahead jumping towards Bullett throwing a foot forward. His leg was easy to dodge but the following elbow was unexpected. Bullett flipped over, rolling with the blow, sliding on his feet. Without pausing, Guy spun on the ground sweeping towards an ankle. Bullett jumped back putting space between them, then leaned in with a full force punch.

Guy caught his fist with one hand and kicked towards his jawline. As Bullett retracted his fist he noticed something neither of them had expected. Both of their hands were bound together. A metal dome encased both of their hands, shimmering in silver and bronze. Guy's foot connected throwing them both to the ground.

Still in a state of surprise, Bullett pulled at his hand dragging Guy towards him. "Stop." Guy half-whispered.

"Do you know what this is?" Bullett slowly shook his head no. Guy smiled.

"It's our golden ticket. This is you, you're controlling it somehow. That must have been inside of you." Bullett continued to pull at his hand.

"How do I get it out, how was it in me?" He started to panic. The orb around their hands wobbled and spiked.

"Woah man, calm down. just close your eyes and see if you can feel it like you did the bars." Bullett's mind wandered back to the bars. He still had a crystal clear image in his mind of their three-dimensional makeup. He focused on his hand, slowly letting the shape and design of this thing form in his mind. Once he felt it fully he tried opening it. Through one squinted eye he watched as it reacted to his mental image and command. It let go of Guy as it formed a glove around Bullett's hand.

"That had to come from inside you. See if you can absorb it somehow." Guy said, pulling his hand away. Bullett could feel it pulsing around his skin, it was warm and somewhat comforting. The metal slowly receded through his pores getting much hotter as it did so, though it didn't seem to burn. In its place, a small amount of blood dotted his skin. He could feel it this time, flowing through his veins. The metal from before dispersed into his system but he could feel the small bits of it as it circled his body.

"That's the key to all of this." Guy whispered. "If we can figure out a way to use that we can escape. The way I see it, if they figured out what you can do they'll have stuff in place to prevent you from using that. However, if… and this is a big if, for some reason they haven't noticed, we may be able to escape soon. But on the chance that they saw what just happened I'd say we have less than 24 hours to make a move."

Bullett nodded in agreement. "The next test" he said, staring at his hand as the metal circled through the small vessels in it. "In the next test I'll use this. I don't know how yet but when I do be ready to move."

Guy put a hand on his shoulder. "Where do we meet up?" Bullett shrugged. "We don't even know where we are."

Guy paused. "Yeah, well we're somewhere, and once we're out we need to be able to find a common point."

~-~-~-~-~

Gabriel leaned back in his chair and propped his feet up on the desk. Ever since he got the promotion he had little work to do. The American dream, being paid to do nothing, and he was living it. An alarm on his computer sounded. He leaned over and tapped a button. "Yes, what is it? I'm incredibly busy." He did his best to sound rushed.

"Sorry sir this is Nettles in the control room. It appears room 57 may have displayed a defensive ability. I've tried all three cameras and can't get a good angle. I am just informing you per protocol sir."

Gabriel plucked at the keyboard and pulled up room 57. As far as he could tell they were just having a conversation about train stations. He clicked the rewind button, stopping just before Leon's entrance. "Alright Nettles, I'll take it from here." He hung up without waiting for a response. He pulled up all three cameras at once, watching from every angle as they interacted with his boss. After Leon retreated he saw the same thing. The small reflection of light for just a moment. Like one of them was holding a mirror. He watched the replay again and again looking from all three angles but could only make out a small fraction of what was there.

He jumped from his seat, a sudden thought striking him. If anyone beat him in telling Leon it could be his job. He compiled everything onto a flashdrive and ran out of his office.

Chapter 12

The wheels were already in motion, Bullett and Guy were already on the elevators towards the final test, plan in mind. Guy stared outside of the glass watching as the pipes intersected and moved past them. "Why are we headed up? Every other test has been down. This is new." Bullett was wringing his hands together, he could feel the metal in his blood. Once he thought about it, he never really lost the feeling. "It doesn't matter where they send us. We have to win. That's really our only option."

Guy smiled, slapping Bullett on the back. "Now you're getting it." They laughed as the light from above poured into the elevator. They crested into the next room and their laughter stopped. They were in a hallway, just a normal, creepy, blood stained, grey-walled, flickering light-lined hallway.

~-~-~-~-~

Gabriel watched a tree outside his window, brown leaves and bare branches swaying in the wind. A storm was brewing outside and he was absolutely ecstatic. He couldn't remember how long it had been since he'd seen outside, much less the rain. He sipped from his coffee;

the toasted pecan bringing back pleasant memories of home. Thunder rolled in the distance. "It's a bit rude of me." He said without turning from the window.

"Pardon?" Leon asked, standing in the doorway.

"This view, this title, this opportunity... they're all your doing and I never even said thank you."

"We don't have time for this. I only promoted you because you're useful. If you start getting sentimental I'll replace you. Simple as that."

"Of course. Your favorite test group should be entering into their final trial right about now. Are we wanting them to pass sir?"

"It doesn't matter really. If they pass they will be moved to another facility for mental conditioning and an even more extensive combat training program. If they lose ... well then none of that will be an option will it? They're very good, but they are not irreplaceable."

"Do you mind if I ask what makes them special?" Gabriel said between sips.

Leon paused. "They're enigmas. They've both tested positive yet we can't find a defensive reaction out of either. And with all of our tests and technology we can't figure out what either of their abilities are. And that

126

makes them an x factor, a variable, and I detest unknown variables. With that said, this final test will either define them or destroy them. Victory either way."

A soft chime came over the computer. Gabriel walked to his chair and pulled up the message."Sir, it looks like the final test has started. If you'd like to stay, I can ask my assistant to bring you a chair and some popcorn."

Leon turned to leave. "Don't patronize me, I'm not a child. I already know where I'll be observing from." Without another word he disappeared through the doorway.

Gabriel turned his attention to the screen, finding a good camera angle to view everything from. A knock came from the door and an armed security guard poked his head in. "Just doing a security check. You doing alright sir?"

Gabriel waved the man away, the final test was starting and nothing was going to make him look away. From his very first day he had imagined what brutality and strength it took to make it through to the end. This was his chance to find out.

~-~-~-~-~

Steam rolled softly from a link in the pipes along the walls above Guy and Bullett as they walked around a corner. "Did you know they're trying to use hydrogen for a heating source?"

Bullett nodded looking around. "The only problem is if the system get's hit too hard it goes nuclear."

"Yeah, they're working on that." Guy turned another corner. "That makes three rights. This is just a giant square. Where's the test?"

"I think it's on it's way." Bullett said stopping. Ahead of them, fog slowly rolled around a corner. With each flashing of the florescent lights it grew closer.

"Think it's acidic?" Guy said as he walked towards it.

"Probably not, but with all the maintenance problems they seem to be having I wouldn't breathe too deeply."

The fog continued to fill the hall in front of them, the light cast shadows throughout like lightning in a storm. Guy continued to walk forwards as it grew thicker, raising an arm to touch the small cloud. Inches before contact he heard the rattle of chains and a small scraping sound.

Guy backflipped out of the way just as a sledgehammer came flying out of the fog, slamming into the wall near Bullett. Bullett watched as a chain attached to the bottom of the hammer became taut and jerked the hammer back into the fog, over Guy's head.

"Looks like it's starting." Guy said smirking.

Bullett frantically looked around the hallway, they needed a plan. Whoever they were against had a weapon, they'd need some sort of defense against it or a weapon themselves. The fog continued towards them, Bullett put a hand against a wall and looked to Guy.

"Keep 'em busy I have a plan!" He shouted.

Before Guy could acknowledge, another hammer shot out of the fog directly at Bullett. Guy grabbed the chain and slammed a foot down on it causing the hammer to launch back the way it came from. As it soared, a second hammer swung sideways slamming into Guy's chest and throwing him into the wall.

Bullett turned at the impact of Guy into the wall, cracking the concrete he fell to the ground clutching his stomach. "Now we're talking." Guy said through gasps.

Bullett jumped up grabbing onto one of the pipes mounted to the wall. He dangled in the air and closed his eyes. He envisioned the bars he had been caged in before. The pipe he was hanging onto weren't nearly as sturdy as the bars were. Praying it would work he focused on the bars he remembered and tried to mentally force the pipe to be as sturdy.

Guy twisted and bent under the onslaught of the sledgehammers, slowly inching his way towards Bullett. As the fog approached, he tried to maintain a safe distance but he wasn't going to let them get to Bullett. He glanced over his shoulder, he was still hanging there with his eyes closed.

Bullett could feel the metal writhe beneath his touch as it rippled and reshaped itself to his vision. It didn't have enough density to work with so he pulled what he could from the length of the pipe. Slowly, it hardened into a solid piece rather than a hollow tube. After a quick mental check for any flaws, he formed a seam between the solid and hollow sections and dropped to the ground, pipe in hand.

As soon as his feet hit the floor, Guy grabbed a fistful of Bullett's shirt and threw him out of the way of a hammer. "Eyes up!" Guy yelled as he kicked another hammer into a wall. The first one hooked his leg on its way back into the fog drawing him with it.

Bullett slid backwards wielding his new weapon like a staff. He charged towards the cloud after Guy. Inside, Guy was in hand to hand combat, blinded by the fog he had to rely on sound. A rattling of chain told him to move, a whistling of wind made him duck. Then a sound he didn't recognize, he was hit in the chest and thrown backwards, colliding with Bullett mid-air knocking them both back out of the fog and onto the ground.

Guy dusted himself off. "I think I've got this now." He pulled Bullett up. "There's two of them, think you can take one?"

Bullett nodded. "One way to find out." He held out the staff. "I think you'll be better with this than me."

Guy smiled, he was better in Noudouken Ryu with a weapon. He wondered what his Sensei would think about this situation. Another hammer sliced through the air towards him. Guy ran forward and deflected the projectile with little effort. It crashed to the floor behind him. As it was being pulled back in Guy slammed the staff down onto the chain and pole vaulted into the cloud feet first.

Bullett stood waiting for a signal. The clanging of metal against metal and a man slid out of concealment like a rag doll. His arms had chains fused with his skin like they had been welded there. Bullett didn't hesitate, he ran to him and grabbed his shirt, tossing him even further down the hallway. Now standing between his opponent and the fog Bullett knew he just needed to delay the man until Guy could defeat whoever was making the fog.

131

Guy used his staff to feel for his surroundings, he swung to either side and above him measuring his placement from each surface. Then, he spun with a leg outstretched and staff angled. The staff hit something directly in front of him, he swung again and it wasn't there. *They must be used to fighting blind. I'm going to have to learn to do this quick.* He closed his eyes and slowed his breath. A palm grabbed his face and slammed him to the ground. He kicked his legs up backflipping out from under them and struck his staff down hitting nothing. *This is gonna be interesting.*

Bullett serpentined down the hallway dodging the incoming thrown weapons, he planted a fist into the man's chest but he rolled with it throwing Bullett off balance. As Bullett continued forward a chain wrapped around his leg. He was jerked backwards and slammed into a wall. The man followed up swinging one of his hammers with both hands in an attempt to crush Bullett's skull. Bullett ducked and swept for his legs, knocking the man to the floor.

Guy followed the sound of footsteps through the fog, periodically swinging towards the source. He mostly met with air but he was slowly becoming more accurate. The rush of wind behind him telegraphed his opponent's movements. He ducked and reached above him, firmly grabbing the arm of his attacker. He jerked forward and rolled his shoulder, throwing his foe to the floor. Still

132

holding his staff in his free hand, he swung down the end into their stomach. A feminine, "Ow, you bastard!" screamed underneath him. Something hit his face and his grip relaxed, the woman slipped away into the fog.

Bullett sidestepped as a hammer slammed down, hitting the floor spraying chunks of concrete and dust. He glanced from the floor to the man, an idea striking him. He ran towards the man ducking under both hammers as they flew by. He grabbed the man by the shirt and rolled backwards kicking him into the air as he flew overhead. Bullett rolled to his feet as the man landed onto the concrete, he jumped high and bent at the knees dropping onto the man's chest. With a groan, the man pulled at one of the chains, throwing a hammer towards Bullett.

Guy was finally getting her movements down, she would semicircle and attack. The pattern was fairly simple but fighting blind comes with a disadvantage. His staff made contact with a leg, he swiftly followed with an elbow to the stomach. He swung again and hit nothing, a surprising blow came from below hitting his jaw. Footsteps retreated as he swung towards the source. He listened for the movement around him, she was behind him this time. He dropped a palm to the floor, cartwheeling towards her. His knee came down on her shoulder, it gave way under the attack with a loud crack.

Bullett backflipped as a hammer pounded into the floor beneath him. As soon as his feet hit the floor he sprinted forward and threw his shoulder into the man, pinning him to the wall. He grabbed his wrist, twisted and turned with a grip on his shirt. The man crashed to the floor and laid there for several moments catching his breath. Bullett didn't give him time to recuperate and slammed his heel down on the man's chest. A thud echoed through the hallway.

Guy used his staff to vault forward with feet outstretched, planting both into the woman's stomach. He kicked off in a back flip, bringing his staff up to meet her jaw. He landed in a spin, sweeping his staff. He made contact with her ankles, sweeping her feet out from under her.

Bullett sidestepped the man's hammer as he haphazardly swung. Drained of energy, the man could barely stand much less fight. Bullett had gained the advantage, he grabbed the hilt of the hammer and kicked into the man's chest, knocking him to the ground. Bullett grabbed the hammer with both hands and brought it down with as much force as he could, planting it right between the man's legs. The hammer hit nothing but the concrete with a loud crack.

The man stared at Bullett silently, blood trickling from his nose. He slowly brought himself to a sitting position. He looked at the hammer imbedded into the concrete, only inches from castrating him. He couldn't help but smile, he finally realized what Bullett's plan was. The floor beneath him splintered and split like glass. Bullett took a few steps back nodding his head to his enemy. "Thank you for your help."

The floor gave way beneath the man's weight, he didn't have the time to scream as he was sucked into the dark void beneath. Bullett watched as the hole spread from wall to wall. The flickering light barely cut through the dust and darkness revealing a catwalk underneath. Bullett almost couldn't contain his joy.

"Guy, time to go!"

Bullett jumped down into the darkness below. Guy could hear the commotion and when Bullett yelled he knew they would be on a timer. He twisted and swung his staff, hitting the woman on the side. He followed up with a kick to the face, knocking her to the ground. He backflipped from where she lay and dashed down the hall into the light once again. It took his eyes a second to adjust but by time he found the gaping hole in the ground he had fully recovered. At least enough to notice the hole and massive damage caused to the surroundings.

Bullett stood on the platform of the floor below, beaming ear to ear.

"We won."

"Not yet we haven't, they'll notice this. We have to be quick."

"Which way? This is as far as I'd planned."

"Haven't you ever seen a movie? We just wreck everything till we find the exit doors."

With that, Guy jumped down on to the catwalk, he stepped over the sprawled out man gasping for breath and headed down the dim path. Bullett put a hand on the railing, the cold metal bringing comfort and the mental image he received seemed to light up the path before him. The groans of their adversaries echoed behind them.

~-~-~-~-~

Gabriel frantically scanned through cameras, amidst the fog and dust he was barely able to make anything out. He periodically switched to thermal view, but with the steam even that was difficult to make out. He had seen the fight in the open was becoming one sided so he had been watching the blind fight with the thermal cameras. One moment it's a heated battle and the next, the man takes off running. By the time Gabriel realized he had completely left the fog he couldn't find him on the cameras. A notification popped up on his screen, with a click the message display overlapped the camera feed.

Cancel the test!-Leon

136

Another message popped up right after.

Go on lockdown! Sound the alarm.-Leon

P.S. Stay away from anything metal.

Gabriel scratched his head. Leon didn't normally communicate through instant messaging. He minimized the window. On his screen the cameras were on a roulette system, something was off about the picture though. After a moment he realized the fight was over and no one was on camera. He frantically hit keys and clicked the alarm. Sirens wailed throughout the building. With a few more clicks a notification to lock everything down went out to all computers.

Security guards ran passed his door, Gabriel jumped to his feet grabbing his coat from the back of the chair. As he swung it around he successfully knocked over his coffee, spilling it over his shirt and pants. Without time to complain he ran out the door into the crowded hall in search of Leon.

~-~-~-~-~

"Take a left at the next intersection." Bullett yelled as he and Guy sprinted through cross sections of the catwalk. The entire place was like a maze, stairs and paths led in

137

every direction but each one ended against a blank section of wall. Bullett had found that the longer he touched the railing the further his mental image had spread of all the connecting metal. He had a map in his head and was using it to reach the highest floor possible.

Guy ran ahead on guard for any dangers. The alarm sounded shortly after they started moving. They managed to stay out of trouble so far but they both knew that wouldn't last forever. As they reached the foot of the stairs Guy dashed ahead. Moving faster than Bullett could keep up with, Guy ran up the railing and jumped into a spin.

Bullett then noticed the two guards standing at the top of the stairs with their backs to them. Guy hooked the staff into one of the guard's neck throwing him backwards down the stairs. Landing on a single hand Guy continued his momentum, like a breakdancer he spun on his palm and wrapped his legs around the second guard's head. As the first guard bounced down the stairs like a rag doll, Guy pulled the second one straight down with all his strength. His head rung out like a bell as it cracked against the stairs. The first guard slid to a stop at Bullett's feet, unconscious but still breathing.

"Well… that was something." Bullett yelled as he bent down over the unconscious guard.

"What are you doing? We don't have time to check on them." Guy yelled.

Bullett held up a security pass he recovered off the guard. "Getting a set of keys."

~-~-~-~-~

Gabriel felt like a fish wading against the current as he pressed through the torrent of people headed for the various safe zones on the floor. Some rooms had already locked down as the metal barriers closed on the most critical rooms first, several of which had people locked in until the lockdown was lifted. As the waves of concerned employees and armed guards dwindled he saw Leon at the end of a hall barking orders at a group of men in uniform.

"... and you three come with me. I swear if they make it out of this building, none of you will be leaving here as free men."

Leon turned and swiped a card at the door behind him. Gabriel started running to catch up.

"Sir. Sir! Leon! It's Gabe sir!"
Leon turned with a crooked smile. "Ah yes, I was going to look for you later. You may pack your things when this is done." With that he let the door swing shut, Gabriel pushed past the guards. He reached for the handle

hearing the lock click before he could turn it. Gabriel stood with his hand on the handle, his mind was struggling to keep up. Behind him something barely audible came over a radio and all the guards took off running with weapons drawn.

~-~-~-~-~

The light was almost blinding as Guy and Bullett stepped out of the darkness into an empty hallway. At least the siren was no more than a loud beeping up here. Guy pressed on towards the intersection ahead, as he poked his head out to check the other directions a voice boomed behind them.

"I've made contact! Hallway B-10"

Bullett turned to see the barrel of a pistol pointed at his chest. The uniformed guard visibly shook as he aimed at Bullett.

"Don't you move, don't you dare move you f..ffreak!"

Bullett had never had a gun pointed at him before, his fear kept him staring down the barrel.

"Guy?" Bullett called. "Any help would be appreciated."

Guy slowly walked forward, he dropped his staff and held his hands up. "Woah man, there's no problems here. We don't wanna fight."

The guard pointed the gun to Guy then back to Bullett. "Both of you stay where you are, I will shoot."

Guy continued to inch his way forward. "Just relax man no one needs to get hurt."

The guard pointed back and forth between the two, unable to discern which was the greater threat. "One more step and.."

His statement was cut short by the blast of his gun, striking Bullett square in the chest. Bullett dropped to the ground. Guy sprinted forward ducking under the shocked man's aim. A second bullet passed over him skipping off a wall further down the hallway. The guard's eyes went wide as Guy got up close. Guy threw an elbow up into the man's arm knocking it upwards. He grabbed him by the wrist and pulled the man towards him, planting a knee into his gut. The guard's eyes went lifeless as the dropped to the floor.

Guy rushed over to Bullett's side, he lay there holding his chest. Guy stood over him in a panic as Bullett writhed.

"It hurt's so much! This is it, this is the end."

"Move your hands, let me see."

"No I can't, I'll bleed out."

"But there isn't any blood yet, let me see."

Bullett stopped and lifted his hands quickly looking at the wound. There was a clear hole in his shirt from the entry but the skin underneath was unscathed. Guy felt a wave of relief.

"Get up you big baby."

He helped Bullett to his feet and examined him. Another hole was in the back of his shirt.

"It looks like it passed right through you without causing any damage." Guy said poking the skin where a wound should be.

"Well.. that's convenient."

"We should move, that cost us time and we weren't quiet."

Footsteps pounded down the hallway towards them. Guy grabbed Bullett's wrist and the staff as they headed the opposite direction. They turned the corner and sprinted down the hall. At the next intersection they turned again, both stopped dead in their tracks as they faced half a dozen guns pointed at them. Behind them they could hear the footsteps of more guards approaching.

"Plan?" Bullett asked while slowly raising his hands.

"I'm thinking." Guy said following suit.

"Nobody move!" Shouted a voice behind them.

Guy quickly glanced over his shoulder then back to the men in front of him.

"Thirteen."

"What?"

"Thirteen men. How many do you want?"

"Ummmm, I don't think that getting shot thing will work twice. Plus I don't think it'll work for you too."

"I know, but we don't really have any other options."

A guard behind them cautiously approached. Putting a gun to the back of Bullett's head, he reached for his arm. Bullett already knew he was about to be handcuffed, he tried to pre-imagine the feeling of handcuffs.

"Six and a half." Bullett stated causing the guard to pause.

"How do you get half of one?" Guy smirked.

"Easy we share one."

The guard slapped a handcuff over Bullett's wrist, immediately metal spikes protruded directly into the man's hand. The guard screamed and before anyone could react, Bullett reached behind him and grabbed the guard pulling him forward into a choke hold. He focused and slowly turned the handcuffs into a makeshift blade at the man's throat.

"Anyone moves and he dies!" Bullett yelled.

"Put your weapons on the ground!" Guy yelled as he took the gun off their hostage and pointed it at him. None of the security moved, they kept their weapons trained on both men. One of the men waved his hand in the air, on his signal both groups slowly worked their way forward. The hostage started crying and begging for them to help.

Bullett searched the hallway, looking for anything he could possibly use to his advantage. In his peripheral he noticed something snaking across the ground. He looked to Guy then nodded towards the hall they had just come from. Guy noticed as well and nodded back at Bullett. Guy lowered his weapon and slowly dropped it and the staff on the ground. He then laid on his stomach and placed his hands on his head. Bullett removed the dagger from the man's neck. He dropped the dagger letting it dangle as the other half of his handcuff. He then turned and put his face to the wall and placed his arms behind his back.

The guards rushed them, throwing Bullett to the ground they piled on both men and began placing them both in handcuffs. They both smiled as a small mist flowed towards them across the floor. The area behind it already shrouded in fog.

"Ready?" Bullett asked as the scraping of chains jingled quietly.

"Always ready." Guy said stifling a laugh.

The security team was too focused on the two men to notice the oncoming fog until it was on top of them. Their chattering and commands dulled to a still silence as their realization of their grave situation became apparent. Within moments Bullett and Guy were covered in the rolling cloud. The men drew their weapons and fired blindly into the dense vapor. Their clips empty, each reached for a spare magazine.

As the fresh magazines locked into place, a sledgehammer slammed into a guard's chest throwing him into several other men. The chain looped around and lassoed another man, dragging him back into the fog. Blood sprayed out from the cloud with a muffled thud. As the men raised their guns again two hammers shot out striking down several others.

A body fell between Bullett and Guy, bloodied and bruised. Guy turned to his side and searched his pockets while the guards were distracted. Upon locating a key he quickly unlocked his handcuffs and tossed them aside. Bullets whizzed overhead as the two groups exchanged attacks. Bullett, having already slipped his restraints, crawled towards the wall. A hammer struck in front of him stopping his movement.

"Plan B?" He asked Guy.

"Same as always." Guy said jumping to his feet and dashing down the hallway.
Bullett jumped up and followed behind, barely dodging another hammer. The security team didn't have the opportunity to turn on them as the attacks began to focus on them again. The sounds of fighting faded in the distance with the two putting as many walls between them and the fight as possible.

Running ahead of Bullett, Guy suddenly skidded to a stop. One of the gates above a door was slightly slumped, raising and lowering itself a few feet in an attempt to shut. It appeared to be slightly off track and unable to close. Guy tried the handle and with the door swinging open, ran inside with Bullett right behind.

Inside, two workers cowered behind a row of computers. Ignoring them Guy circled around to a computer.

"What are we doing? We need to leave!" Bullett yelled in a whisper.

"Hold on something may be useful here, I just need to figure out a way into their systems."

"You aren't going to be able to just hack these."

"Who said anything about hacking… I'm gonna guess."

"If you guess wrong you could set off an alarm."

"I'm gonna go with… Bubbles." An incorrect password message showed.

"Stop man, we could always just ask."

"How about Goobledeflecker?"

Bullett turned to a woman mumbling to herself.

"Ma'am I'm not going to hurt you. I just need your username and password."

She shrunk away at his gaze but shakily answered.

"Use..user i..is H2V0K and password." She paused, blushing. "Banana hammock, capital B one word."

Guy smiled. "That was gonna be my next guess."

He quickly typed both in and browsed through the various applications. Bullett knelt next to the woman.

"Thank you, do you happen to have any flash drives or anything?"

She nodded and pointed to a desk. "Third drawer."

Bullett smiled and went to retrieve one.

"Dear God they have terabyte flash drives!"

"Good we're gonna need it." Guy said scrolling through files. "They have dozens of people on file, data regarding some sort of biological strain, and schematics of buildings. Look here," He pointed to the screen. "this one looks like it's in Dallas and they have another in Austin."

"Copy it, we don't have time to search everything. Just get the files and let's go."

Guy popped in the flash drive and began copying data. A fist pounded on the door and both men looked to each other.

"Is everything alright in there?" A voice bellowed behind the door.

Bullett turned to the woman with a finger on his lips. She nodded and glanced to the door.

"They're in here! Help!" She screamed. Guy grabbed Bullett and ducked behind a desk just as the door slammed open. Armed guards rushed the room, guns pointed in every direction. Guy snatched the flash drive from the computer and tucked it into his pocket.

"Get out of here." Guy whispered.

"What? How?" Bullett responded in kind. The guards started sweeping the room, fingers on the trigger.

"I'll distract them, just get out and lay low. I'll come find you."

Before Bullett could respond Guy jumped up landing on the desk. As all guns pointed towards him he swung his staff hitting guns and arms alike causing a spray of blood and pistols across the room. "Go!" He shouted, flipping into the midst of them. He pushed one man backwards, knocking several others down and turned to fight the ones to his back.

Bullett knew he couldn't waste the opportunity, half-crouched, he ran around the desks and dashed over the fallen guards into the hallway. He turned and didn't look back as he made a beeline away from the chaos. The shouts echoed behind him as the fight intensified. Ahead of him he could see the end of the hall. A single person sat in a corner staring out a window without a gate or bars. Beside him a plain door stood unguarded.

Bullett slowed to a walk, cautiously approaching the man. He wore a plain suit, though it appeared to be stained with coffee. Bullett stopped in front of the man, unsure whether he was injured or not.

"You ok man?"

He continued staring forward, he mumbled something under his breath but his eyes never wavered. Bullett looked to the door, same as all the rest save for a sign reading "In case of fire". He grabbed the handle, instantly the image of the inner workings flashed into his mind. Before he even tried to turn it he knew it was locked. With a bit of concentration he managed to move the locking pin enough to allow him to open the door.

Bullett stood over a staircase leading down, he turned to the man in the suit who only mumbled something to himself. Shrugging, he stepped in and shut the door behind him, sliding the locking pin back into place. The staircase was quiet, Bullett could swear he could hear his heartbeat echo. No guards or personnel anywhere in sight, he made his way down.

Traveling down several floors, he followed the emergency signs. As he reached the ground floor he stepped into a large lobby area, abandoned and unguarded. To his side large doors led to the outside. He could already smell the fall wind stirring the dead leaves from their trees.

Suddenly the building shook like an earthquake causing several tiles to fall from the ceiling. Bullett ran through the metal detectors, ignoring their alarms, and through the exit. As he burst through the doors the building shook again spewing flames, smoke, and glass from several windows.

Bullett backed away watching the fire. Somewhere up there Guy was trapped, if he wasn't dead already. His legs were weak, nothing felt real. This moment shouldn't have been possible, the chain of events leading here felt like a dream. Another explosion took out a corner section dropping bodies and equipment several floors to the pavement below.

A single helicopter circled the building, high above the heat and destruction. Bullett decided to run, he didn't want to be seen alive nor captured again. He turned, looking for a way out. Beside the building he noticed a fenced in parking lot with vehicles scattered about. If he could manage to get inside one he could possible get the ignition to work without a key.

151

Above him a window shattered. He looked up and froze. Mid-air, Guy had the coffee stained man by the collar with his feet planted in his back. They fell together like a skateboard and skater, Guy using him to break his fall. On impact Guy tucked and rolled with the momentum, sliding to a stop on a single knee. The other man was not quite as lucky, landing face-first from several stories up and painting the pavement with his life.

Bullett struggled through his shock.

"What.. the… hell was that?"

Guy smirked.

"I found the boiler room."

He spoke as if it explained everything up to this point. Bullett looked from the dead man to the burning building then to Guy. His mind pushed it all aside to be processed later. "Let's get out of here man."

Guy looked around, surveying for a way out.

"Hey! I think that's my car over there!"

He pointed to the parking area.

"Of course it is."

Bullett threw his arms up and resigned himself to go with the flow until he could find a logical stronghold. Guy rested his staff across his shoulders as the two walked to his car, their prison in flames behind them.

---------- **Chapter 13** ----------

Hours later the two found themselves parked in a high school parking lot. Guy handed Bullett a wrapped burger as he slid into the driver's seat. Both starving, they ate in silence. Exhaustion had caught up with them once their adrenaline wore off. Though tired both were well aware they were nowhere near out of the woods yet. Bullett finished his meal first, he looked out of the missing window beside him.

"What's the plan?"

"Well we can't stay here and we can't go home. So our options are either hiding for the rest of our lives or… now stay with me here, we can take these guys out."

"But we don't know who these guys even are or where their base is."

"Yeah, but we do know where two other buildings are." Guy held up the flash drive.

"We know there's one in Dallas and another in Austin. The problem is once they find out about this they'll up security. If we can take these out simultaneously then we'll have a bit of breathing room and cause a bit of chaos on their end."

"Well true, but in order to do that we'd have to split up, find these buildings on our own and then take them out solo within days of each other."

"Ok, well what if we set a date to attack?"

"That might work but do you really think we can each handle this alone?"

"Who say's we'll do it alone? There's got to be others out there like us who aren't captured. Even if there isn't, if we train hard and prepare we should be able to at least do critical damage and get out."

"Alright, you know this is crazy right? But, I've been close enough to dead so many times now that that's not even scary anymore."

Bullett leaned his chair back, watching the clouds as they passed. Guy finished his burger, throwing his trash out of the passenger window.

"So… which one do you want?" Guy asked, rolling the flash drive across his knuckles like a poker chip.

"Dallas, I know the area a bit better and if I'm lucky I think I know of a few good places to pick up someone else like us."

155

"Alright, then I'll take Austin. There's this pizza place I've been dying to try. Now that that's solved, how long do you think we have?"

Bullett ran some scenarios in his head. He didn't quite remember agreeing to the plan but he really didn't have any other options.

"Assuming we're up against the government or other entity with limitless resources... A week, any longer and the risk is too high."

"Alright, a week from today we make our move. Second order of business, how are you going to get there? I'm not gonna drive you there and waste time on my half."

"I figure I'll just hop on a passing train somewhere in the woods."

Guy put the flash drive in his pocket, started his car and made his way towards the highway.

"Just be sure to practice, we can't be amateurs going in alone. Pick a bar fight or hunt down some druggies if you have to."

"I'll practice. Just watch, next time we meet up I'll be able to beat you in a fight."

Guy laughed. "It's not me you're going to need to beat. How are we gonna find each other after this?"

Bullett drew a symbol in the dust on the dash resembling an altered question mark.

"This is kinda my logo, I use it for everything. Stay in Austin and I'll tag some stuff with it and leave some clues."

"You could always... I dunno, call me."

"Well we don't know if that's being monitored and I don't have my phone."

"Just in case I'm going to write it down for you before I drop you off."

The car grew silent, both were thinking the same thing. This is the first trial they'd have to undergo alone since they both met. While they hadn't known each other long they'd become reliant on the support of one another. Would either fare well without the other?

Bullett did his best to take a nap while Guy tried finding a good spot along the train tracks to drop Bullett off.

After a while Guy pulled to the side of the road and shook Bullett awake.

"About a quarter-mile into those woods is a track that heads towards Dallas. I checked the schedule and a train should be coming through here in the next 20 minutes."

Bullett rubbed the sleep from his eyes, noting the sun had almost set. Sneaking aboard shouldn't be too difficult. With the various tests he'd been through this almost felt too easy.

Guy handed Bullett a piece of paper.

"This has my number on it. Call me if you find out anything important or if things get too sticky. If that doesn't work, leave me a sign."

Bullett nodded. "Alright. I'll try to leave something in Dallas in case you finish before me." He got out, gently closing the door behind him. He wasn't sure if he was ready to go on this adventure alone.

"Wait." Guy called. As Bullett leaned back into the missing window, Guy grabbed the staff from behind his seat and extended it towards Bullett.

"Take it, just in case."

Bullett held a hand up to decline.

"Keep it, I can always make another."

"Alright, but promise you'll make it to Austin. I'll kick your ass if you die before me."

With a forced smile Bullett slapped a hand on the top of the car.

"I Promise, but I expect the same from you."

He turned, walking into the tall, dark grass. Guy wanted to say something to reassure his friend. Both were well aware that they may never see each other again. In the distance the horn of a train blared, marking its position. Bullett broke into a sprint, shadows enveloping him.

Guy watched until he was out of sight. With a sigh he started the engine, turned on the headlights and u-turned back onto the highway. He had a long, lonely drive ahead.

---------- Chapter 14 ----------

Guy made his way down the road. In light of the recent events, he felt more vulnerable now than he could ever remember. Alone in his car, he was left with nothing but his thoughts as night turned to day. Driving from city to city, he could see small changes all around him. Even the air itself felt more tense and heavy. How many others were like him? What caused all this insanity in the first place? What if he failed to bring down the facility in Austin? All these were questions that ate at him, like a splinter he couldn't quite pick out.

To try and pinpoint his focus, he began thinking of what exactly he was going to do when he arrived. His best option was to hope this facility was set up like the previous one. If faced with an all-out assault, the military would be called in on him within the hour. Even if that wasn't the case, it wasn't as though he had an army to assault with. His biggest fear was that they had already been alerted to the breakout he and Bullett had just made. They will surely have upped their security substantially. A few people may still be able to sneak in undetected, however, if he could manage to swipe an ID card. Any plan he could come up with was a longshot with huge risk. Even if he was able to get inside, he would have to fight his way back out again. There was no way releasing all those prisoners would go unnoticed. What if the captives he rescued couldn't fight. Even if they did help, would it be enough to fight a building filled with highly trained government agents? Or worse still, what if there was no one left alive to rescue?

Lost in thought for hours, Guy didn't even notice when he crossed the Austin city limit sign. He was quickly brought back to his senses though when his two-lane road merged with a six-lane highway. He pulled into a hotel parking lot and killed the ignition. *I need help. That's all there is to it. I can't risk going in without backup.* Suddenly struck with inspiration, he took out his phone, plugged it into the car charger and downloaded the first police scanner application listed. He sat and listened for what seemed like hours more before he heard anything with promise.

"...We have a robbery in progress on Parmer Lane. E-Z Pawn pawn shop. All available units respond..." The voice from the local dispatch seemed to echo within the car. "Be on the lookout for a hispanic male, mid twenties, tattoos on both forearms. Suspect appears to have left through the east wall..."

"Dispatch, this is unit 5519 responding. What do you mean he left through the wall? Are any civilians injured? How much collateral damage was done to the building?"The officer's tone went from official to hurried and nervous in seconds.

"Negative 5519, no damage to the structure and no injuries at this time. The shop's manager stated she witnessed him walk *through* the east wall."

Guy hurriedly threw the car into reverse. He wasn't quite sure how he was going to track down this guy, or even what he would find if he did. He just knew this was his best shot so far. His eyes darted back and forth from the road to his GPS as he navigated the big city's road system. Once he exited onto Parmer Lane, it was easy enough to find the pawn shop he was looking for. *Hispanic male, mid twenties, tattoos on both forearms.* His mind repeated the few clues he was given. *If this guy can walk through walls he is going to be a hard one to catch. It's not like I can corner him.* He drove along through the neighborhoods situated behind the store.

His app blared with chatter again. "Possible sighting of suspect headed south on Willow Wild, reports of multiple break ins. No injuries reported at this time."

Guy followed the directions and turned down Willow Wild Drive. He couldn't help but notice the big city seem to fade as the quaint neighborhood gave off a small town feeling. Houses became more scarce sooner than he expected. With nothing really pointing him in either direction, he took a left at the next intersection he came to. Trees dotted the winding path along both sides.

He thought he had chosen the wrong road until the trees stopped and a clearing opened up into an open softball field on his left. Police cars sat scattered throughout the small parking lot, taking it over with their presence and flashing lights. He slowed his car and scanned the field. It appeared that the neighborhood children were in the middle of a game, interrupted by police officers forming an encasing circle around a man in a black hoodie.

Without giving his plan much time to process, Guy turned the car around and sped toward a makeshift path leading up to the ball field. He cut his tires to the right and pulled the emergency brake, sending his car spinning. Releasing the brake he shifted into reverse and, still mid spin, reached over and opened the passenger side door. In what seemed like one well planned move, the car scooped up the fugitive. The stranger closed the door and righted himself in his new seat. As soon as the door closed, Guy shifted back into drive and hit the gas pedal.

The two were back on the road and through the neighborhood before the officers could make it back to their patrol cars. Neither spoke as they made their way across town and pulled into the back of the parking lot of one of the many roadside hotels. Guy turned off the car, flung open his door, and ran around to the bed of the car. Tucked beneath his spare tire were two new license plates. He quickly replaced the old ones with the new and threw the old in the nearby dumpster and walked back to meet his new friend. He sat back in the driver's seat and turned to the passenger, who sat motionless.

"Nice driving back there," the man said, breaking the silence.

"Was it worth it?" Guy replied

"Was what worth it? I don't do things unless the reward outweighs the risk."

"Saving your ass back there. Was it worth it for me to put the entire city's target on my back?"

The passenger reached into the pocket of his sweatshirt and pulled out a stack of bills, halved it, and threw one half to Guy.

"That's not what I meant. I don't need your money. I need your help. I'm Guy by the way."

"I go by Shift to anyone who needs to call me something." Shift paused in thought. "I'm not really the soldier-for-hire type."

"Then it's a good thing I'm not hiring you. You owe me."

The two stared at each other for a few moments until they both started to laugh.

164

"Alright Guy you got me." Shift said still laughing. "What is it we're doing?"

Over the next hour, Guy told Shift his story. He left out a few details, giving only the information he felt was needed. Periodically, Shift would interrupt and ask Guy to fill in some blanks, but mostly he sat and listened. When Guy was finished, he realized he forgot to ask a very important question.

"What is it, exactly, that you can do?"

"What do you mean?"

"I mean you have to have some sort of ability right? You couldn't have evaded all those cops without some sort of skill. So what are you, some sort of teleporter or something?"

"Nah man this isn't some video game."

"Hey, after some of the things I've seen people do, you'd be surprised."

"I've had skills before this freakshow shit even started. It just found a way to improve perfection." Shift said smiling and flexing. They both laughed. "I can vibrate the particles of objects at a high frequency, it lets me pass right through them."

Guy sat in silence. He thought he had picked up some two-bit thief with powers but he now realized this guy was smart. He would have to watch his back much more closely now.

"So what is it you can do?" Shift asked.

Guy thought for a moment. "Honestly I'm not too sure how to explain it. I'm just... more in control. Like I can tell my body exactly what I need it to do."

"Wow... that's a shitty power. I learned to do that when I figured out how to walk." Shift said with a smirk.

"Oh, ha ha... you're hilarious."

They rented two adjoining rooms in the hotel after deciding the money would be well spent for two reasons. One, they needed a space bigger than an El Camino to plan out their next moves. Two, they would need a good night's rest. Who knew how long it would be before they were able to stop and sleep comfortably again? They talked strategy for over an hour, each of the ideas shot down for one major flaw or another.

"We are going around in circles. How are we supposed to break into a building when we don't even know where it is?" Shift said, finally asking the question they had both been thinking.

"I don't even know where to start. It could look like anything" Guy replied. They sat quietly, both lost in thought.

Shift broke the silence, "I think I might know someone who can help. He isn't cheap, but he's the best."

Shift made the phone call and an hour later there was a knock on the door. Shift unlocked the bolt securing the entrance and in walked an unexpectedly short man, further dwarfed by the oversized messenger bag draped across his shoulder. Thick glasses sat on his face, making his eyes look disproportionate to the rest of his body. He walked over to the table and unpacked a laptop and various boxes and cables.

"Guy, this is Wifi, the city's undeclared computer prodigy." Shift said pointing to the new person in the room, "If there is a record of anything out there, he can find it."

Wifi sat at his workstation and stared at the screen. "So what is it you're searching for?"

Guy started into his story again but only made it a few sentences in before Wifi interrupted. "Oh you're looking for the hidden research laboratory. That shouldn't be too difficult. I have had a general idea at where it's been tucked away for some time now, just no reason to do any further digging. Possible occupational hazards and all."

"Wait, you know about this place?"

"Conspiracy theories have been popping up all over the web about some underground research company doing all sorts of experiments. Everything from creating human puppets to accelerating photosynthesis to hyper-mature local flora. Most guesses are illogical and preposterous of course."

Guy had never heard anyone speak like Wifi. He had a somewhat thick Texas accent, which would have been normal to hear if it weren't for the Oxford-like way he enunciated his vowels. He spoke rather quickly, pausing only long enough to punctuate his sentences by pushing his glasses back to the top of his nose.

"It is a simple matter of collating all the known data, then separate fact from fiction." Wifi continued, "I should have rough coordinates in a few hours. I would be done sooner if it weren't for those damned signal towers giving me spotty reception."

"Works for me. I'm not really in any hurry to get shot." Shift said flopping back on the bed he had been sitting on.

Wifi ignored his comment, his fingers blazing over the keyboard. "Now for the matter of my payment. Highly classified intelligence isn't cheap."

"How "not cheap" are we talking?" Guy asked warily, "I have a little in savings but probably not enough to cover what you're about to do."

"Oh I don't need your money. The masses only assume that money rules the world. In fact, information is a much more valuable currency."

Guy realized what he was getting at. He thought for a few moments and reached into the pocket of his jeans, removing the flash drive. He walked over and placed it on the table in front of Wifi. "If it's information you're looking for then this should be more than enough payment."

"What is this?" Wifi asked skeptically.

"It's data I downloaded from their computer system before me and my friend escaped. The data on that drive is all top secret."

Wifi plugged the drive into the USB port closest to him and began picking through files. His face lit up like a child at an amusement park. "This is more than enough."

A few short hours of sleep later, they had their location. It was now or never.

---------- Chapter 15 ----------

Bullett jumped from the moving train, sliding to a stop on the pavement. He glanced around but no one seemed to notice his entrance. With the sun rising, the city had just begun waking up. He had hopped from train to train all night trying to make his way to Dallas without a map. His luck improved when he happened upon two other stowaways who were more than happy to give him directions.

With a tire shop, dentist's office, and mexican restaurant all lined up next to each other, amidst hundreds of houses, Bullett knew he found the perfect hiding place for a random building. The next step would be to find it, though the growling of his stomach would disagree.

Bullett quickly thought up a plan, walking behind the tire shop he grabbed a stray length of chain, dangling from a support beam. He wrapped it around his arm as he continued around circling towards the dentist's office. On either side of the office door, two plastic plants served as decoration. He scooped up one of the pots and dumped out the faux plant. He continued down the street, allowing his mind to picture the chain.

The chain itself was new to Bullett, up until now everything he had touched was like a solid piece. Even the doorknob had solid pieces held in place by other pieces. This was a different beast altogether. It felt like dozens of worms with their own movements and reactions.

He walked for a block or two until he found a busier area, with people jogging past and others heading into the various shops, this would be as suitable as any other. Using two fingers he punched a small hole in the bottom of the pot. He fed the links of metal through it, stuffing a few links from the other end into his sock. He found a spot out of the way and sat cross-legged, dropping the rest of the chain into the pot. Then he closed his eyes and focused on reshaping a section of chain.

After a few minutes of awkward glances and obvious attempts to ignore him, he was ready to start his act. As a mother and daughter walked past the young girl pointed to him. "What's wrong with him mommy?" She asked, tugging at her sleeve.

"He's sick honey, it's rude to point, just leave him alone." She tried walking faster.

Bullett smiled. "Wanna see a magic trick?"

"Sure!" The daughter yelled to her mother's obvious disgust.

"We don't have any money, sorry." The mom tried to hurriedly walk away but the daughter planted her feet.

"Look mom a snake!"

Bullett had his hand just above the pot with a metal snake head underneath it swaying as though hypnotised. The eyes were hollow and further down the body was just chain but the head itself looked to be a cobra. Bullett said some made up words and held his palm in front of the snake which in turn rested its chin across his fingers.

"Wow!" The girl exclaimed, inching closer against her mother's protests.

The pure excitement of the child attracted the attention of other people walking by. As Bullett continued to perform, his mastery over his creation increased. Before long he was able to give it a realistic ripple to the scales as it moved and even a tongue that flickered from time to time. The crowd's excitement peaked when he bit off its head and put it back with no visible harm done to the creature.

He sat there for about an hour, collecting the small bills and coins in the pot as they were laid at his feet. For a final act he made the snake balance a quarter on its nose before curling back into the pot. The audience clapped and questioned his methods as well as complimented his act. With a few dismissive comments

173

about magicians and their tricks, he sat back until the crowd dispersed. It didn't take long for the streets to return to normal and his presence to be forgotten.

He stashed the pot behind a bush and stuffed the money in his pocket. Patting the wad of cash, he continued down the street searching for something filling and cheap. Before long he was chowing down on a burrito, wandering the streets aimlessly. He knew his first priority should be shelter but he wanted to get a head start on locating the building. His only clue to go on was it looked like a brick house with boarded windows and a broken garage door.

Several hours, two sodas and an ice cream cone later, Bullett had wandered down street after street looking for the facility to no avail. His search would have to end for the day if he was going to find a place to sleep for the night. Thunder rolled in the distance, almost insisting a roof would be needed soon.

Bullett made his way towards a highway, counting his money hoping he could afford a hotel room for the night. A hand suddenly grabbed his shoulder pushing him towards a wall. Bullett turned to see a knife staring him in the face, a very erratic and mostly-toothless man shook the knife in his face, spitting his every word.

"Your money or your life…"

He stepped back slightly and held out a hand as though the outcome was obvious. Bullett was a bit stunned, his first day back in civilization was almost enough to forget about the past weeks… almost. His time spent fighting for his life day after day was hard-wired at this point. He would not go down here, he had a friend he made a promise to. This man would not be enough to make him break it.

Bullett's arm shot forward, palm outstretched inches from his assailant's face. The man staggered backwards, upon seeing the empty hand he beamed a toothless grin. He stepped towards Bullett, knife prepared to strike.

"Your weapon or you life." Bullett said, stopping the man momentarily. Keeping arm's length away he lunged the knife forward aiming for Bullett's gut. Like lightning the metal snake worked it's way from Bullett's sleeve and down his arm, it lunged at the man and wrapped around his throat before he could react. His knife sunk into Bullett causing immense heat to radiate from the entry.

The snake coiled around his throat like an anaconda locking in a vice. The links of chain still in Bullett's hand like a leash. The man quickly realized his mistake and released the knife to claw at his throat. Gasping for breath his face started to turn several shades of red.

Bullett pulled the knife from his stomach and tossed it to the ground. "Wrong choice." He made the snake grip tighter causing the man's eyes to bulge. His legs gave out, he continued to claw only able to force a squeak as a plea for mercy. Staring into his eyes Bullett wanted to force this man to suffer, he wanted to watch the life fade from his eyes, he wanted to be the strong hero he'd dreamt about… but he couldn't.

The snake released its vice grip and retreated back into Bullett's shirt, wrapping again around him. The man collapsed, pale and gagging, as Bullett walked from the alleyway and onto the street. He glanced around to see if anyone noticed him, he tried to look as normal as possible as he continued to search for a hotel. Tiny droplets of water sprinkling down warned of the oncoming storm.

~-~-~-~-~

River held up a toy pony to the window, pretending it was flying through the streets of Dallas. The tinted windows obscured most of the details though, the imagination of a nine year old more than made up for it. Her dad, dressed up with suit and tie, talked on his cellphone about something boring right beside her. She drowned out his conversation with one of her own.

"Hewwo widdle Wiver." She said in her best pony voice.

"Hello Mr. Sunshine, how are you today?" Her adult voice sounding like a children's show's host.

176

"I'm wonderful!" Her pony said, sliding across the back of the seat.

"That's good Mr. Sunshine! Have you met daddy yet?" The pony trotted across his leg.

Her dad covered up his phone.

"Not now honey."

"But I wove you!" She held the pony up to his face.

"I said not now." He used his stern voice, pushing the toy away.

Defeated, River turned back to the window and watched as the sky cried on the city. Buildings and people passed outside as the rain continued. A sliding window in front of them rolled down and a man in dark shades looked at them through the mirror.

"Sir, we're almost there."

She watched as one of her daddy's employees rolled the window back up. Just before he went out of sight she stuck her tongue out at him and quickly looked out the window again. She hated them, they weren't allowed to play with her and always got her in trouble. Even worse, they never really talked to her... most people didn't talk

177

to her, everyone was so busy talking with her daddy that they forgot she was there.

Sometimes she would sneak around the house pretending she was a ghost, her and Mr. Sunshine would hide under a sheet away from the eyes of daddy's workers. They would peek through cracked doors and try to listen to people talking without being caught. Sometimes she would whisper things and make spooky noises to scare them away. They got caught a lot though, she blamed Mr. Sunshine for being too loud.

She remembered when she was younger daddy used to take her to the park a lot. She got to go on the swings and slides and daddy was nice. That was before the men in glasses, before Mr. Sunshine, and before mommy left. She'd gladly trade the pony for a day at the park with her dad again, even if she never got to see mommy again. Mommy left a long time ago. River struggled to remember her face.

River could barely reach her drink in the cupholder ahead of her. She strained forward, just able to touch it with her fingertips. Without looking, her dad grabbed the bottle and passed it to her. She took a big gulp of the water and screwed the cap back on. She slid the bottle behind her. She could find a place to put it without needing daddy to help, like an adult.

The car came to an abrupt stop and the window rolled back down. "We're here sir." The man got out and opened the door for her dad while people outside cheered and took pictures. He smiled and waved as the door closed on River's view. Her door opened and a different man in glasses held his hand out to help her from the car, he smiled. He was the first one she had ever seen smile. She wondered if he was nice, or if he would offer to play with her. He held a large black umbrella over her to protect her from the rain even though he was getting wet.

She took his hand and hopped from the back of the long car, holding tightly to Mr. Sunshine under her arm. As he lead her forward she tried looking at all the people over the hood of the car but wasn't quite tall enough to see anything but the top of people's heads and umbrellas. Ahead and behind the car she was in were cars that looked exactly the same. Perhaps they also had kids in them like her. She splashed in a puddle as they walked around the car, throwing mud on the man's pant leg. She expected a scolding but looking up he was smiling at her.

They rounded the car and she could see daddy taking pictures with people. She was jealous that daddy spent so much time with other people, she furrowed her brow and whispered to Mr. Sunshine.

"I bet he doesn't take *them* to the park."

People shoved each other aside trying to get close to him. Several of her dad's staff were spread through the crowd, but she knew who they were. She'd seen them all before. Suddenly the sound of a loud firework went off. It scared everyone, even daddy, he ducked down to the ground. Other people screamed and ran in every direction. Another firework went off but she didn't know where they were.

The man holding her hand pulled her up by her arm, it hurt, he ran to one of the other cars and threw open the back door tossing her in. She didn't know what to think.

"Where's daddy?" She asked

"He'll be ok, we have to go-" Suddenly a wet mist sprayed from him splattering on her pretty new dress and face. She reached down and touched it, looking at it she noticed it was red. She'd scraped her knees enough to know what blood looked like. She screamed a shrill, ear-splitting cry as he slammed the door. He dove into the driver's seat and started it up. Tires squealed as they peeled away, slamming into the car in front of them as they drove off.

Tiny spiderwebs appeared across the windows as they drove away but she didn't notice, she was still screaming. The car swerved in and out of traffic, they bumped into more cars as they sped across the city.

River was tossed around the car, Mr. Sunshine fell to the floorboard and disappeared underneath one of the seats. After several minutes of chaos there was a screeching of tires as they slammed into a pole, catapulting River to the floor.

Groggy, River struggled from the floor back into the seat. She looked to the driver's seat and saw it was empty, smoke billowed from the crumpled hood and the window was barely hanging in it's frame. The door beside her popped slightly, slightly misshapen, it was forced open to its loud protests.

Bent at the waist, the driver extended his arm towards River. She could tell he was in a lot of pain and his hand held his stomach but did little to keep the blood from seeping through his fingers.

"We have to put a band-aid on that right away or it'll get infected!" She half-yelled.

With his free hand he held her back and forced a smile.

"Don't worry about me I'll be fine. Now listen, I'm not going to be able to go with you. There's some bad men coming and you need to hide."

She tried to protest but his hand gripped her shoulder, silencing her as a tear slid from under his disheveled glasses.

"Run and don't look back. Get as far away from here as you can and don't trust strangers. We'll come find you and bring you back soon ok?"

She sheepishly nodded her head, still staring at the blood dripping to the ground. He glanced around not familiar with the area. Luckily traffic was light with the event happening a few miles away. He saw a playground in the distance, he rotated River to face it.

"Go hide in the playground, I'll send help. Don't trust anyone if you don't recognize their voice."

He turned her back to face him, his skin growing a sickly pale.
"There are bad guys coming and they'll try to trick you, I need you to be a brave girl and make your daddy proud. Can you do that for me?"

Tears were already streaming down her face, she wiped at them smearing his blood. She was trying to be brave but the entire situation was confusing. She wanted to make daddy proud though so she'd do this, like an adult, to make daddy happy.

The man turned her back to face the park and gave her a tiny push. He had grown weak and leaned against the car.

"Go!" He forced out. "Help will be here soon."

She headed towards the park, intermittently sprinting and shuffling her feet. A proper lady doesn't run but he told her to run. Her confusion came up with two simple rules for her. Run and hide. She'd figure out the rest later.

She hadn't noticed the sun setting, the clouds were much too thick to see it. The sprinkles falling down were getting bigger. The rain was about to begin.

~-~-~-~-~

Lightning flashed across the sky and thunder rattled the city. Everything seemed to vibrate with electricity except Bullett. He sat on a dumpster in an alleyway, as the rain poured down he stared at the cracked concrete beneath him.

Having managed to find an hourly hotel, he was able to get about four hours with the money he had left. The first two was him trying to sleep but he was plagued by nightmares every time he closed his eyes. Visions of Guy being torn apart, of his own head on a pike, he dreamt of horrific mutations and blood stained floors. He didn't sleep much.

The second two hours he used to practice his ability, which he had started calling his powers in his mind. He was able to turn the snake back into a chain and to a snake again with ease. He managed to turn it into various weapons and with trial and error found that if he focused hard he could sharpen a blade with only a thought. The very arrangement of particles was under his command. The problem was if he had to focus, during a fight or stressful situation he wasn't sure he could make such transformations. He decided he'd stick with the snake until he got better.

He left the hotel, exhausted and broke, looking for a foothold in this city. He searched road after road for several hours until the rain began to pour down in sheets. His depression reached an apex and he stopped to get his thoughts in order.

Sitting in an alley staring at the ground he knew he'd need money, a way to search faster, and food. His stomach growled but he suppressed it. He had no way to get food until he sorted this out. He thought about mugging someone, not for all their money but for enough to survive. A vision of the man trying to rob him at knife point flashed in his mind.

He couldn't bring himself to bring that kind of terror to an innocent person. He was hopeless. He couldn't even kill some meth addict who **should** have been killed. But he had never killed anyone. Up till this point everyone he had fought had enhanced strength and the like, so he was able to go all out. But against someone without powers, even a murderer… could he kill them?

Water dripped from his nose into the growing puddle below. Something was scratching at his mind like claws. He couldn't quite figure out what is was. Like his mind was screaming at him. Around the corner footsteps splashed towards him. He was surprised he could hear it over the thunder and rain, he hadn't realized how sharp his sense had become.

A young girl ran by in a full sprint, with terror in her eyes she was too short of breath to scream yet all the same Bullett could hear her screams. They echoed in his mind and reverberated a fear and emotion that words couldn't express. A dark and menacing emotion gripped his heart and strangled the bravery.

As she continued past the alley, she turned and made eye-contact for a single moment. He wasn't sure if it was the look in her eyes or in his head but the word "help" yelled through every part of him. Lightning flashed above, highlighting the blood and dirt soaked into her dress.

Bullett wasn't sure what action to take as she ran from view, her footsteps fading. Several more footsteps approached, heavier and slower than the girl's. Several men strolled by, the look of depravity rampant on their faces. They did little to hide the look of lust and insanity

185

as they held various weapons with pride. One let a bat drag behind him, another had a crowbar across his shoulder and a third kept flipping a knife in and out. All five kept their eyes on the girl, not even so much as glancing towards Bullett.

A sense of dread washed over him as he observed it all, like seeing the events leading to a train wreck. He kicked off the dumpster landing with a small splash. He turned the corner watching the group catch up with the girl. The one with the bat took the initiative and ran forward hitting her in the stomach with the end. She dropped to the ground on her hands and knees, barely remaining conscious. The one with the knife grabbed her by her hair and dragged her towards a nearby apartment complex.

The apartments themselves looked to be abandoned with some windows boarded up and cracked sections of wall. A scaffolding to the side indicated some sort of maintenance had been taking place but was left unfinished.

The men circled the building and entered from a side doorway, ducking under the boards blocking their path. The entire time they moved the girl never spoke or screamed, and still, Bullett could feel her pleas in his head. From his spot in the darkness of the alley he felt like she was staring at him as they drug her away. Her eyes piercing through to his core.

In that moment he had a realization, like suddenly all of the thoughts swarming in his mind connected and formed a clear picture. He now understood why the villains in games hated all of humanity so much and why some people could look death in the eye and smile. He stared at the apartment, expressionless, lightning flashing and rain pouring, he noticed neither as he calculated a plan.

Inside the men laughed as they drug their catch behind them. Still pulling the girl by her hair they filed up the stairs, squeezing past broken furniture and cardboard boxes, kicking aside the occasional water bottle or beer can. Several floors later they entered a dimly lit room. Past couches with exposed stuffing and appliances of various working conditions they threw the girl into a wire dog cage. A nearby electric lamp was turned up revealing minor burn marks, blood stains, and multiple weapons speckled throughout the room.

As soon as she landed, River turned on her heels to flee only to have the door close in her face. A nearby lock was snatched and promptly latched over the handle. A few of them circled her with lust-filled grins.

"She'll make a great toy." One said as he flopped onto the couch.

"Hopefully she'll survive longer than the last one. The boss wasn't too happy with her."

A few nodded, as they took various spots in the room in waiting. One leaned against the window, passively watching the lightning reflect off the puddles below.

River sat still, hands on the bars, watching everything silently. Tears rolled down her face though she was trying her best not to cry anymore. She already knew it wouldn't help, it would most likely make things worse. She learned more about adults in the past 24 hours than she had her entire life. And she was scared, adults were supposed to be nice people but all she found was monsters.

He was coming though, he told her to be strong and she was trying. She knew if she could be a little stronger she'd see her dad again. And if that meant trusting someone new, even though she wasn't supposed to talk to strangers, she was going to try.

A loud crack echoed from the concrete below.

"What was that?" One said, too preoccupied with using his knife to clean his nails to be bothered to look away.

"Don't know, looked like a tv." The man next to the window pressed his face against the glass in an attempt to see directly below him.

"Open the window dumbass."

He complied, struggling to pull up against years of rust and paint. The window slowly screeched up a few inches at a time until it finally gave enough room for him to poke his head out. The rain sprayed into his face making him squint against the water and wind.

"It...it looks like a microwave." He extended out further, trying to get a good look at the ground floors below.

"Where would a microwave come from?" One of the other men asked, grabbing his bat.
"Well it had to come from-" His sentence stopped short with a loud crack.

All of the men jumped to their feet as their partner's body dangled limply from the windowsill. Several parts of his spine were broken leaving him in awkward angles. This would have been fatal even if his head hadn't been completely caved in by a falling night stand.

Weapons at the ready a few slowly approached the window to check on their friend. One ran to the door to peer through the hole into the hallway while the last ran through the hall and disappeared into another room.

Thunder rolled, shaking the room, glass and metal rattled for several seconds amongst the static of rain and thunder. As it subsided a thud came from a few floors above. The men reached their friend and pulled him inside, checking his pulse one simply shook his head silently to the others. Another thud above them and the sound of things being violently thrown around. Again, something banged from the next floor louder than before.

Everyone scrambled to defensive positions, each gripping their weapon of choice tightly. The pounding continued, drawing ever closer until finally it sounded as though it came from inside the room; each bang shaking the entire room. River gripped the bars until her knuckles turned white, she kept telling herself to not be afraid. She couldn't help it though, the fear emanating from the men was almost too much for her to bear. Her one saving grace was the anger and hatred she felt boiling inside, it was enough to ground her and keep her eyes open for what was to come.

The repetitive banging finally stopped, complete silence followed. No one dared to move, something was coming and they had no idea what it was. River looked to the ceiling and smiled, he was here.

Another sound shook the entire room like an explosion, the roof started to collapse in a mixture of plywood, dust and debris. Bullett dropped into the middle of the room landing on a knee with a fist to the floor. Around his wrist was a giant metal bracelet several inches thick, it slid it's way up his arm resting just under the shoulder.

As he rose to his feet the men throughout the room snapped from their stupor and attacked. Bullett quickly examined the room, seemingly ignorant of his approaching attackers he met the eyes of River. With a slight nod in her direction he remained stone faced as he turned to attack.

River watched as his fist made contact with the closest man, the bracelet shot down his arm to his wrist as his fist connected with the man's chest. The impact was sickening, multiple crunches accompanied his chest caving inward, causing his body to curl in on itself and collapse several feet away.

A bat struck him across the back of his leg and he wavered slightly, before the men could take advantage he jumped into a spinning kick breaking another's collar like a twig. As the bracelet worked it's way slowly back up his arm, Bullett used his free hand to grab the back of a third man's head and brought it down to his rising knee.

River was in awe, she'd never seen such violence nor felt such a protective rage. She recalled a time when daddy had stepped between her and a mean dog that was trying to get her. He had gotten bit and it bled a lot but he didn't even cry. The man fighting in front of her reminded her of daddy. He was getting hurt but he was doing it to protect her.

Bullett was struck in the back with a chain, ripping his shirt and skin. Staggering forward he turned just as a follow up swing hit him in the throat. The man with the busted nose grabbed him from behind holding Bullett's arms to his side allowing for the other man to attack again, busting Bullett's lip. Bullett stepped forward as though the man holding him were nothing more than a backpack, he headbutted his attacker knocking him to the floor. With little effort, Bullett dove backwards landing on top of the man causing him to release his grasp. He rolled backwards off of the man and punched down onto his face, the initial impact breaking his nose and several teeth. His bracelet slammed down onto his wrist causing a second shock wave, destroying the facial bones in a spurt of blood.

The last man, shakily rose to his feet. Glancing around at his dire situation he visibly faltered in his conviction. Bullett's eyes burned with hatred as he stepped towards the man. Bullett ducked under his wide swing and rose up, gripping the man by the throat and holding him off the ground. He was sure of himself this time, he would squeeze the life out of this man and watch as he faded away.

"Stop it you're scaring him!" River yelled.

Bullett snapped from his blood lust. He dropped the man, who fell choking and coughing, to the ground. Staring at his hand, still suspended in the air, he tried to piece together the last few moments. He looked at the man on the ground gripping his throat, then to the girl in the cage. She looked back, terror and hope both discernible in her expression. He gripped the lock, closed his eyes for a moment and it unlatched.

The door to the back room banged open as a man of herculean proportions charged through. He paused to survey the scene, eyes locking on Bullett knelt in front of the cage. Grabbing a long piece of rebar from the ground he sprinted towards Bullett. Before he could react he skewered him on the pole. The metal had gone straight through with almost a foot of it, soaked in blood, sticking out of his back.

Bullett dropped to his knees, the only thing keeping him upright was the pole pressing against the floor. He still hadn't processed everything that just happened. A burning sensation in his chest and freezing at his back. River shook the cage, her voice cracking.

"No! Please get up, don't let him get me!"

Her voice was distant to Bullett. He knew what happened to living things when vital organs were pierced. He was more mad at himself than sad, he couldn't even save a little girl from a giant. How was he ever vain enough to try to be a hero.

"Please!" River begged. "Don't die!" She sobbed, death was a new concept for her. Within the past few days she'd heard the word quite a few times but everyone had a different meaning for it. Ultimately, she figured out enough to know it was an end of the person, where they couldn't do anything anymore.

Bullett sighed, a thought occurring to him. *I can breathe... how?* The muscle bound man laughed a deep laugh and tossed Bullett across the room where he bounced off a wall, landing in a heap on the floor. He ripped the door off the cage and threw it over his shoulder on top of his own allies.

"Now come here pretty little thing, daddy wants to play."

She backed up as far as she could in the cage.

"I don't wanna play with you!"

He gripped the front of her dress and jerked her from her entrapment.

"But I want to play with you."

He smiled and licked his lips.

A flick of wind puffed past his face and the girl fell to the ground, still gripped by his hand. He looked toward the source of the disturbance to find blood pouring out of where his arm once was. Bullett stood behind him, rebar still sticking out of both front and back. With a katana-like sword in his hand, his bracelet gone. The giant struck him with his remaining arm, Bullett launched backwards through the wall into the adjoining room.

River struggled free from the unattached arm, running to hide while he had his back to her. Bullett spit out blood, while the rebar seemed to get pushed further through him, it was almost as though he was unaffected by it. However, he couldn't leave it sticking out like that. He kept his eyes on his adversary while concentrating on the metal. It slowly split open and pooled on his chest and back, seeing this the giant stopped his advance. The metal surrounded his off-arm, giving it the appearance of golden armor.

Having had enough, the behemoth dropped his shoulder and ran forward with a roar, crashing through the wall with a trail of blood in his wake. Bullett put his armored arm up and sidestepped. Gripping his already weakened shoulder, it didn't take much for Bullett to bring the man down like a charging bull. He slid a ways, stopping when his head hit the wall. Giving him no chance, Bullett jumped on top of him and slid the sword through his back into the floor below. Once it was deep enough he split the sword on both top and bottom into a T shape, anchoring the beast to the floor.

Quickly surveying his surroundings he noticed the man that ran during the fight in the corner, skull crushed with large indents from what could only be the giant's fingers. Beneath him the muscle bound man tried pushing up with his one arm, roaring and straining against the anchor.

Bullett knew the flimsy metal wouldn't hold him for long. He spotted a wallet on a stand next to the door, grabbing that he ran into the main room looking for the girl. She poked her head from behind the couch.

"Is it safe?"

He held out a hand to her.

"Almost, we need to leave. What's your name?"

She gingerly approached him taking his hand.

"River."

She looked into his eyes without fear, her gaze inconsistent with her tattered and blood stained clothes.

"Come on River, let's go."

Bullett smiled as he led her to the stairs, they moved as fast as River's feet would carry her. Above them they could hear the struggles of the man as he fought to get up. Several floors down they could hear the crashing as the giant mass of muscle tore through the apartments looking for them. Bullett picked up River and ran to the streets below disappearing into the veil of rain.

---------- Chapter 16 ----------

It had been dark for a few hours when Guy and Shift reached the location Wifi had given them. It was a live music bar on 9th Street, so normal the two thought they had the wrong place. After a moment wrestling with the decision, Guy thought it best to leave his staff in the back seat. *No point in drawing unnecessary attention to ourselves.*

They walked in and sat at the bar where Shift bought the first round of drinks. It took them an hour before they noticed anything out of place. More people were entering than were leaving, yet the bar never filled.

"Shift, care to take a look around?"

"I'll let you know if I find anything worth telling." Shift said as he finished his drink and turned toward the bathroom.

Shift walked into the bathroom and entered one of the stalls. He pressed himself up against the wall and stepped through to the other side, finding himself behind the bar near a dumpster. He stepped back through and went up to a section of wall near the sink. Once again pressing against the wall, he walked through into what looked to be the manager's office.

Shift began shuffling through drawers to no avail. He leaned against a corner of the desk and noticed a small square in the top was more smooth than the rest. He ran his fingers along the length of the desk and across the square. Lights danced throughout the square before turning a deep red and fading away completely. This seemed like just the thing Guy was looking for.

Guy was downing the last of his second drink when he saw his friend walk back out of the bathroom. Shift sat down and picked up his now refilled glass. He nodded to Guy as if thanking him for the drink and turned to the bartender, "Excuse me, my colleague and I are looking to rent some office space in the area. Any ideas?" With an understanding nod, Guy got up from the bar and turned toward the back hallway.

"This is Austin man," the man responded while pouring a beer, "turn a corner and there's something for rent. It ain't gonna be cheap though."

"Good point. Thanks anyway."

Guy was navigating the tables when the sound of shattering glass made him turn around. The broken mug distracted him just long enough from him to run directly into a waitress. "Oh sorry excuse me. My bad." She stared at him annoyed and went to clean the mess, muttering "Stupid drunks" under her breath.

Guy turned down into the seemingly abandoned hallway next to the bathroom and quickly found the office he was looking for. To his surprise it was unlocked. He walked in the door, trying to appear as a drunk stumbling into the wrong room, just to find it empty. He wasn't sure what he was looking for or even if he took the hint correctly.

It was a few minutes before Shift walked in the door behind him. "It's over here on the desk." Shift said pointing at the spot he touched before. He ran his hand across the top again like he had before expecting lights but none came. "I don't know. That's exactly what I did. There were lights and everything."

"Wait you already tried opening it? I bet this entire place is on lockdown at this point."

Guy had just enough time to finish his sentence before the floor behind the desk shook and began sliding into another section of floor. Both men stood shocked but Guy was the first to speak, "Ok as cliche as that is, that was pretty badass. The stairs leading down into darkness are a little unnerving though." They shrugged and started down the stairs.

About the time they could no longer see the next step, the nearly invisible lights mounted to the walls on either side of them turned on, illuminating their path and showing them a long corridor ending at a "T" intersection. The two reached the end only to find more empty hallway to either side. Guy turned left and kept walking.

After two rights and another left, Guy stopped confused. Out of habit he put his hands in his pockets. His right touched something unfamiliar vibrating ever so slightly. He pulled out the object to discover an earpiece. After a moment of inspection he put it in his ear. "...these unobservant bastards are going to get themselves killed."

"Hello?" Guy responded as quietly as he could.

"Hello? Guy can you hear me? This is Wifi."

"Yeah I can hear you. When did you put this in my pocket?"

"That isn't important right now. I've been monitoring the database for these guys. I was getting gold until about 10 minutes ago the entire site shut down. Everything is suddenly behind thousands of layers of firewalls with some pretty sophisticated encryption, almost as if they caught someone tapping into it. I know it wasn't me."

"Shift hit some sort of control panel when he first found one of their offices. The timing adds up, but it let us down so it must have worked."

"Oh it worked. They know you're there. Run!"

Guy turned to run and realized Shift was nowhere to be found. He sprinted down the hallway and spun to the right and froze. There to meet him were a dozen guards led by the most intimidating woman he had ever seen.

She was at least six feet tall by what he could guess and clad in a near skin-tight military uniform adorned with what seemed like a hundred medals. She walked up to Guy with a confidence gained only from never being defeated. He stood frozen as she got closer. Something about her terrified him but still he stood there, unable to act, waiting to see what she would do next.

Guy mentally prepared himself for a fight. She was close enough to reach out and touch him but Guy was still unable to move. Though his instincts screamed at him to react, her overwhelming presence rooted him in place. Another step in, the woman ran her hand down the side of his face. "Such a noble attempt. Loyalties are a curious thing. So easily wavered."

Guy felt something try to burrow into his mind. Focusing all his attention, he pushed it back, fighting the intrusion. He managed to keep it at bay, barely noticing the guards run past him and down the hall he hadn't explored. The sounds of doors slamming and orders being barked bounced off the concrete walls around him.

In the midst of the chaos building all around him, Guy was beginning to lose focus. The control of their captain was quickly growing from a manageable splinter in his mind to an all consuming force. He turned to see Shift rounding the corner with a dozen of the infected now freed prisoners. Gunshots rang out from behind the group, a single bullet hitting a young girl square between the eyes. The shock caused Guy to lose the final foothold he had on his own mind. He dropped to his knees, hands over his eyes, as he lost himself in the sea of images being bombarded into his head.

As soon as the gunfire began Shift dove toward Guy, using the bend in the hallway for cover. He saw the bullet connect with the girl he just saved. She couldn't have been more than twelve years old. He turned to Guy expecting him to jump into action amid the pandemonium, only to see him on the ground clutching his skull. He was about to run to him as Guy stopped screaming and rose to his feet. Shift's newly renewed hope was quickly snuffed out as his friend blankly walked passed him and into the crowd of prisoners. He watched in horror as Guy approached one of the men defending them and snapped his neck.

Dodging the spray of lead, Guy swiftly jumped between each of the prisoners executing them without blinking. He had killed all but five before they noticed what was happening. Two of the men grabbed him by either arm and hurled Guy back down the hall where he came and sprinted toward him to finish the job. Before they could get the jump on him, Guy was already on his feet. He ran at them, dropping to his knees and sliding between them. Guy struck out at one of the prisoners, who was fighting off the guards with a broken mop handle, connecting precisely above her elbow. The bone gave way with a sickly snap that could be heard even over the gunfire. He grabbed the handle before it hit the ground and swung it in a wide arch around, slitting the woman's throat with the jagged edge.

At the end of his swing, Guy lunged at the leftmost of his two assailants. The man punched forward. Guy grabbed his wrist and used his arm as leverage to pull himself closer, smashing his forehead into the man's face. Blood sprayed out of the man's nose as Guy landed crouched on the ground. He immediately jumped back up, thrusting the broken mop into the underside of the man's jaw. The handle went clean in, sliding through the roof of his mouth and ending six inches out of the far side of the man's skull.

It all happened too fast for the second man to react. He watched as his roommate dropped to the ground into a sticky crimson pool. He stood still and focused his energy, hardening his skin. Guy jumped at him, striking blow after blow into his now near-steel epidermis. Grabbing his shoulders, the man slammed Guy hard into the wall, bouncing his head hard off the concrete corridor, stopping only once he was sure he was unconscious.

The scene played out so quickly Shift barely had time to process. Seeing his friend out cold, he lept to his feet and ran at the captain. He lunged at her from a full sprint. Steeling himself, he phased his body through hers, solidifying on the other side. Shift threw himself into a spin and punched the captain at the base of the spine. She was momentarily thrown off balance but swiftly regained her composure and turned to fight her assailant head on.

The two fought for several minutes, neither able to land a blow of any real effect. Though both combatants were too preoccupied to notice, the fighting around them had stopped. They also failed to notice the tough-skinned man coming toward them.

The captain blocked a jab and was following up with a right hook when a massive hand struck the side of her head, palming it like a basketball. She was thrown headfirst into the same wall Guy had been crumpled against. In only three more strikes, the captain was defeated covering the wall in a new coat of red paint.

Guy started to stir as Shift was kneeling down to check on him. After a few moments taken to catch their breath, Guy was able to stand. "What the hell happened?"

"You went berserk back there. One minute you looked like you were fighting the world's angriest headache and the next you were taking out the prisoners." Shift said, still getting over the shock.

"I killed prisoners?"

"Yeah. It all happened so fast. I had no clue what was going on. It's over though, we won."

"We didn't win! You're telling me I slaughtered innocent people and are trying to pass it off as winning? If anything this is all my fault. If I wasn't stupid enough to think I could take on an army, none of this would have happened!"

"Yeah you're right. None of those people would be dead … yet. There is no telling what kind of twisted shit these guys would have done to them. From what you've told me they would have had to fight to the death anyway. At least this way more than two of them made it out alive."

"I guess so."

"That crazy bitch had control of your mind or something. You weren't yourself."

"Ok, so how did I end up on the floor?"

206

Shift stood silent and pointed behind Guy. "Him."

Guy turned and saw a hulking man. He was at least six feet tall with shoulders broad enough to rival the stoutest linebacker he had ever seen. The man approached him and held out his hand. "The name is Knox. I suppose I'm responsible for at least part of your headache. I thought things might go a little more in our favor if you were unconscious."

Guy begrudgingly shook Knox's hand. "Thanks ... I think."

Shift spoke up to break the awkward silence that followed. "Anyone else ready to get the hell out of here?" The two men unanimously agreed and all three started down the hall back the way they had entered not long before. It wasn't long before they realized the place had been deserted. Guards no longer patrolled the halls and even the bar patrons left their drinks half full.

"I can't thank you guys enough." Knox said once they had all passed through the front door back into the public. "I don't think I would have made it out. If there is anything either of you ever need, don't hesitate to find me." After a brief farewell he walked back up the street and out of sight.

Again, Shift broke the silence. "Now what?"

"I don't know about you but I could use a nap and a shower."

The pair went back to the hotel and paid for another night. They went to their respective rooms. Guy took his shower and stumbled to his bed while, one room over, Shift snacked on the travel sized bags of chips and beef jerky he raided from the vending machine and pulled back his covers. Both were asleep as soon as their heads hit the pillow.

When Guy awoke it was dark again. He had slept through and into the next day. He could hear a conversation through the door joining the rooms. Guy rapped on the door and was greeted by Shift, still mid sentence. Wifi was sitting at the table, once again behind his computer, discussing the flood of recent online discussions regarding the appearance of strange people with "superpowers".

"Here's another one, about a man that invaded a domicile by coming through the toilet."

"How is that even possible?"

Wifi shrugged. "Hydrodynamics?"

Guy interjected. "What exactly are we talking about?"

"It looks like there are a lot more people like us than we thought, and they aren't nearly as quiet about it." Shift replied.

"More people going missing?"

"No. Stores being robbed and homes being invaded. Can you believe that someone would use powers like these for something so selfish?"

"Um, we met because you were robbing a pawn shop and you only got away specifically because you were using your powers."

"Yeah but that was before. I'm a new man now."

"That was like three days ago!" Guy said laughing. "In fact there are beef jerky wrapper all over your bed. How did you get those?"

"Well I … Look *now* I'm a changed man. And that isn't the point. These people are attracting attention we don't need."

In the midst of the conversation, Wifi was digging through his bag. He pulls out a small metal cylinder and sets it on the table. "I hate to interject but I have a job for you. If I am going to keep digging for information I am going to need more access than I have now."

He hands the cylinder to Shift. "This device is an amplification relay. If ya'll can hide this in the central communications building of an internet service provider I can use those same databases as a primary starting point. Anything that hits the cloud I can access instantaneously."

"So we just drop it somewhere out of the way?" Shift asked rolling the device in his hand.

"Precisely, then I will take care of the rest. Sneak in, drop the relay somewhere nice and hidden, and I will take care of the rest from my end." Wifi looked at them over the rim of his glasses. "If you leave now the building should be mostly empty and you won't have to assault anyone."

Guy and Shift glanced at each other and Shift flopped back onto his mattress and opened another jerky stick. "Nah, I'm more of a morning person."

Chapter 17

River sat on the bed kicking her feet, watching cartoons on the hotel tv oblivious to the world. Bullett watched the morning sun glinting off the cars as they drove past. He flipped a driver's license through his fingers. He wondered how it had come to be in that apartment. *Markus Finch, did he own the apartment or was he a victim of those monsters? Either way I owe him.* He glanced to River, giggling at some robot pirate flying a spaceship. *And her?* She still had blood and dirt smeared on her face and dress, he was lucky to sneak her through the back entrance without being noticed. *I need to figure out who she is and what's going on with her but... I'm also on a timer.*

"I already told you I'm River." She said, eyes never leaving the tv.

"What?" Bullett asked, she answered a question he never asked.

"I'm River, daddy was in trouble and his friend drove me and we crashed and he got hurt then I was alone."

Bullett paused. *Is she traumatized or just talkative?* Before he could open his mouth to speak, River continued.

"I don't know what that first one is but I like talking." She turned and smiled at him, it would have been cute if she didn't look like she crawled from a grave.

"River… can you hear me?" Bullett asked her, carefully watching her expressions.

"Mmhmm" She nodded. "Ever since the park I can hear everything, even the stuff people don't say." She turned back to the tv giggling at the hyjinx.

So you're telling me that you can read my mind?

"Maybe, I can just hear what you're not saying is all." She stuck her tongue out at him. "I know my dress is dirty but I don't have another one."

He palmed the money in his pocket contemplating buying her a new one but, he couldn't be walking around the streets with her looking like that.

"I'll stay put and watch tv, I won't go anywhere I promise." She held out a pinkie. Knowing all too well the seriousness of a pinkie promise, Bullett shook on it.

"I'll be right back, don't go anywhere." Bullett half-sprinted down the stairs towards the exit.

An hour and a half later he returned with clothes and pizza. He walked in the door, surprised to find her in the exact spot he left her. She smiled as he walked in the door.

"Daddy doesn't let me watch tv much at home."

Her eyes fell to the bags of clothes first and she squealed loudly.

"Are those for me? What all did you get me?"

"I wasn't sure what size you are so I got a bunch of different stuff, and some clothes for me too."

He sat down the bags and separated their clothes.

"First things first.." he had already been planning on how to bring it up without sounding creepy but she finished his thought for him.

"I know I know… take a bath before I try them on. And THEN you were gonna give me pizza."

She sounded exasperated, like they had been arguing all day and she finally conceded. Without another word she gathered all of her bags and waddled towards the bathroom door barely able to see over her luggage.

At the sound of the faucet turning on, he grabbed a slice of pizza and plopped in front of the tv. He was never one to watch the news as he was a firm believer that most of it was made up or wrong. But he was willing to watch it if only to gain tiny nuggets of truth. His life had changed drastically in just a few months and yet, the world didn't seem to be that different. He couldn't believe nothing had changed.

At first, most of the stations he found showed the same boring stuff they did every day. A robbery here, a shooting there, a celebrity caught with drugs, a plot to assassinate the president, a fire… nothing out of the ordinary. About the third time he saw a station reporting a fire outbreak in Texas he caught a glimpse of something in the flames. He found a fourth station showing the same footage and he finally caught it. Inside the flames a person stood watching the sky, they were engulfed in the fire but they weren't reacting.

He was about to grab the remote when the bathroom door swung wide open. River waltzed out, her hair wrapped in a towel larger than she was used to. She barely remained vertical as she put her hands on her hips and proudly asked.

"How does it look?"

She was in one of the outfits Bullett purchased, a black dress with white floral designs on the fringes. She tried to spin causing her towel to unravel itself falling over her face. Bullett laughed, finishing the last of his pizza.

"If you can read my mind, why would you ask?"

She pulled the towel back revealing a single eye.

"Cause sometimes a lady likes to hear nice things."

She obviously picked that up from someone else but Bullett's mind still held the image of someone on fire.

"You look nice River... listen we need to talk."

"I know already, we need to find daddy and there's people with superpowers and you're worried about you friend."

Bullett was a bit taken aback, while he believed she could read minds he wasn't sure how deep she could reach. He was also prepared for a long drawn out conversation but she beat him to it. The whole mind reading thing was going to take some getting used to.

"River, let's try talking the whole thing out so I can be sure we're on the same page ok?"

"Ok!" She plopped down onto the bed, trying to fix her towel back onto her head.

"River… first thing first. Who are your parents and do you know where they are?"
She thought hard for a moment, visibly straining her mind.

"Mommy is gone and daddy got taken away. It's ok though, one of the men in glasses said he'd come find me."

She did her best to put on a happy face but she was bad at lying. Bullett could tell something bad had happened and based on the information he had, finding her father would be near impossible. River fought back tears, snapping Bullett back to attention, he'd have to keep his mind in check around her. He wouldn't be able to hide the truth from a telepath.

"Well then, let's work on something else." He tried taking her mind off of it. "When did you start reading minds?"

"Yesterday, I'm not really good yet."

"Just yesterday huh? Do you know what made it start?"

"Nu uh." She said, giving up on the wrap and deciding to towel dry her hair.

"Ok, last question. Where do you want to go?"

She stopped rubbing her hair and looked at him judgingly.

"The park?"

Bullett smiled and nodded in response.

"We can go to the park. I'm also trying to find a certain house so we can walk around afterwards, and we've got enough money left over that we can go for ice cream too. After that though we will be really low on money so we'll have to get some more."

"What about daddy?" She questioned.

"You said he'd find us right? Let's try to be sure we're both safe and stuff before we work on that. But I promise if there's a way to find your dad we will." He rubbed the top of her head, skewing the towel over her face. "Now, it's my turn to take a shower. Watch some tv and eat some pizza then we'll head to the park after I'm done."

River perked up, she had forgotten the pizza. She ran and grabbed two slices, making a sandwich and flipped through the channels to find more cartoons. Bullett showered and dressed into less battle-worn clothes, in addition to a shirt and pants, he had bought a hoodie to help conceal his face. He grabbed all of the blood-stained clothes from the floor and tossed them in the trash. In one of the clothing bags he also had a

217

messenger bag, he grabbed all of their remaining possessions and stuffed them into the bag for easy travel.

After they both finished off the pizza they watched a few more cartoons, Bullett doing his best to take his mind off of all of his worries. Not for his own sake, but to keep River from knowing everything he knew. He, as an adult could barely handle it, he wasn't sure how all of that information would affect a child.

They checked out of the hotel and headed towards the park the front desk clerk informed them about. River was so excited she couldn't stop talking. The whole way she informed him of Mr. Sunshine, the man in glasses, being a ghost, and her dad. From everything he could gather from her ramblings, her dad was important. But he could have been anything from an actor or mayor to a mob boss or even the President himself.

He set that all aside in his mind to be worked on later, they arrived at the park and played for hours. She wanted to swing, slide, climb and run on everything possible. They tried hide and seek at one point but Bullett came to conclude that telepaths cheat even if they don't mean to.

After several hours, the sun was beaming down on them, Bullett suggested a snack and River reluctantly accepted the ice cream bribe. She didn't want to leave but she did like ice cream.

They found a shop down the street, while waiting in line River excitedly pointed out all the different flavors they wanted to try, eventually settling on strawberry and kiwi. Bullett picked out vanilla for himself. As he was paying, River tugged at Bullett's sleeve cupping a hand beside her face. Bullett leaned in for her to whisper to him.

"He knows where that house is."

Before he could ask her if she was sure she just nodded her head. He questioned the clerk, being as specific as possible and after an awkward conversation mixed with a few white lies about buying the property he finally had the information he needed. They walked back towards the park discussing their next plans.

"River, where I'm going will be dangerous."

"I know, there's a lot of bad people there that are going to try to hurt you."

"That's not the part I'm worried about, I don't wanna take you in there if you might get hurt too and I have no idea where to take you that will be safe."

"I wanna go with you." She nibbled on the cone without looking up.

"But I can't take you, do you know what happened to us in there?" He hoped he was grasping the strength of her powers.

"Mmhmm, most of it. But you'll keep me safe like you did with your friend."

"But River, I don't know if I can keep you safe."

She opened her mouth to speak but stopped to shove the rest of the cone in her mouth. She stopped mid-chew and turned around looking towards the street.

"Someone is looking for us."

Bullett turned, a cop car had just parked and two officers were approaching.

"Maybe they found your dad and they're coming to get you." Bullett absentmindedly theorised.

As the cops approached, Bullett took River by the hand and they both walked towards the cops. As they got closer, one immediately called for backup on the radio and they both pulled their guns. Instinctively, Bullett pulled River behind him and held up his hands.

"Is there a problem officers?"

"Get on the ground now!" One shouted pointing towards the ground with his gun.

"Woah! What's going on here?" Bullett feigned innocence, knowing it could be one of a dozen reasons for them to behave aggressively. He needed to know where he stood and how bad it was.

"Step away from the girl and interlace your fingers behind your head!" The second officer commanded..

"Alright you're both telling me to do different things." He held his hands out towards them. "I'm unarmed, what's going on here?"

Sirens sounded in the distance, it wouldn't be long before more cops showed up. River peeked from around Bullett looking at the cops, they reminded her of her dad's men. Back then she didn't know what they were thinking, but the men in front of her had intentions of shooting regardless of Bullett's actions. She tugged at the back of his shirt, he glanced over his shoulder quickly.

"What is it?"

"They want to hurt you." River whispered

"I see that." He said staring at the guns, tires screeched down the street as the cops continued to shout contradicting commands.

"No… I mean even if they get me they still wanna shoot you. They think it'll make them famous."

"I see, just stay behind me. What do they want with you?"

She paused as she searched through their flurry of thoughts.

"They both don't care if I live or die. They think they'll still be heroes."

Her heart sank as she said those words, she'd been used to being neglected but never before had she felt her life was worthless. Bullett's blood boiled, he couldn't stand to see a child harmed. While Bullett didn't consider himself inherently "good," he lived by a set of certain rules and as such would defend this girl even if it cost his life.

"I said get on the ground bitch!"

The first officer yelled as he slowly inched forward. Multiple cars pulled up, blocking off the street. Some with shotguns and others with pistols drawn, poured out of their vehicles. Using their cars as shields, they trained their weapons on Bullett who stood with arms still in the air. River tugged as his shirt again.

"He said…. biiiiitch." She muffled her voice in the typical fashion of a child repeating a known swear word.

Bullett meant to say a snide remark but an explosion from the cop's gun cut him short. Pain shot through his gut and out his back as a bullet passed through him, behind him River screamed in pain. Everyone froze seeing the blood spray from River as she fell to the ground clutching her shoulder.

Bullett dropped down beside her, ignoring the guns behind him, he pried her hand away to inspect the wound. The police again shouted commands but they fell on deaf ears. Luckily the bullet passed straight through her, as she sobbed the wound started to coagulate and the bleeding slowed at a much faster rate than it should have. She curled into a fetal position crying for her dad, this flipped a switch deep inside Bullett.

Standing, Bullett turned to face the officers approaching him, slowly taking off his messenger bag and dropping it beside him. Arms at his side with an expressionless face he walked diagonal to them. The threats and commands went unheeded to Bullett, in his own world, as he drew their aim from her direction. More shots were fired, however, this time they didn't pass through him. The heat was near intolerable, dropping him to his knees. A few headshots dropped him to the ground.

The closest officer approached to check his pulse, as soon as his fingers touched flesh Bullett's hand shot up grabbing him by the wrist. Bullett, quick as lightning, jumped to his feet simultaneously, using his free hand, he thrust his palm into the cop's elbow snapping it like a twig. Not giving them a chance to respond, he spun around and threw his shoulder into his victim's torso, using the leverage to throw him towards the street.

Before the body hit the ground, the police opened fire again. This time Bullett was determined to stay standing, he continued his march towards the officers, still carrying a blank expression. With a quick burst of speed, he darted the ten feet towards the next officer, absorbing the bullets like a sponge. River screamed in terror, eyes shut tight with hands over her ears. Hand outstretched, Bullett grabbed the officer by the face and slammed his head into the earth beneath him crushing his skull. As he rose a katana-like blade slid from under his sleeve up his palm. Several cops had emptied their clips and reached for spares, their fear clearly visible in their eyes.

Another dash and Bullett stood between four officers, blade in hand, with precise slices he downed them all before they could finish reloading. Calls came from multiple men for backup, claiming the men dead and Bullett a monster. He almost laughed out loud, they were the monsters in his eyes. The scene quickly deteriorated as the bodies fell one after another until all that was left was Bullett, breathing erratically and tattered, standing in a pool of blood. His work finished, the blade disappeared back into what was left of his sleeve.

River had stopped screaming, she simply rocked back and forth mumbling to herself. Bullett snapped from his blood lust and rushed over to her. Multiple sirens wailed in the distance, Bullett didn't have the option to comfort her. Throwing his bag over his shoulder, he picked her up in his arms and ran as fast as he could leaving hell in his wake.

For hours the two hid inside a storage unit several blocks away. With daylight fading Bullett left River alone just long enough to search the other units for supplies. He returned several times bringing a gas-fueled heater, a pile of blankets, and a first aid kit. He hung up a blanket, using it as a curtain so they could both change and discard their bloody clothes. Once changed, Bullett used alcohol pads to clean River's wound. They were both surprised to find that not only did she not have any signs of damage but, there wasn't any scar tissue present. It was as though the wound never happened.

River barely spoke the whole night, she had a day that would traumatize anyone, child or adult. Bullett was proud of her, he never had a little sister but if he did he'd want her to be like River. It didn't take much to get River to sleep, once she curled up in the middle of the pile of blankets next to the heater she was out. Bullett, however, couldn't sleep.

He replayed the events of the day over and over in his head. He had lost control of himself in a way he couldn't have imagined before. The blood of a lot of people stained his soul now, not that he regretted saving River but the lives of multiple men were taken because of his actions. Fathers, brothers and husbands… all died by his hands. He recalled their last words, begging for help from a monster. Was he a monster? He didn't care, he would become the most powerful monster there is if it meant stopping beasts like them.

Somewhere in the back of his mind he felt a calming whisper. "You did well, you should rest." He knew he was alone but he searched for the voice anyway, River rolled over in her sleep, talking in her dreams.

"I love you too daddy."

He smiled as he covered himself with the only spare blanket and thought to himself. *If this is what it means to be a monster then I accept.* Closing his eyes he still heard the distant sound of sirens and helicopters. For the first time in a long while he slept peacefully.

Morning came in gracefully, the sun glinting off the morning dew with a crisp chill blowing in the wind. The heater had run out of fuel some time in the night and River was the first to notice. She shook Bullett, waking him from his deep slumber.

"I'm cold."

She forced through a yawn while rubbing an eye. Bullett opened one eye and stared a moment, taking too long to remember where he was.

"Turn the heater up."

"I tried but it's broken."

She sounded defeated, she had tried for almost an hour to warm up and couldn't take it any longer. She hated asking for help because it made her feel like a child but she was out of options. Bullett dragged his bag to him and searched through the pockets, he counted the money they had left.

"Alright, how does hot-"

"I love hot chocolate!"

She shouted, suddenly full of energy. She hugged him quickly then paused, she forgot to wait for him to finish his sentence and hugged him when he wasn't ready. She felt the awkwardness from him and apologized for both. He dismissed either being a bother, even though she knew better. They both put on their jackets, Bullett being sure to pull her hood up as well as his own.

"We can't really let people see our faces after yesterday."

"Why not? They were the bad guys and you stopped them!"

Bullett sighed.

"You and I know that but the news won't show it that way. I hurt people, and that makes me the bad guy."

"But you're not!"

River wined. Bullett chuckled and patted her on the back. He was worried about appearing in public so soon after the spectacle he made, hopefully it was still early enough that no one had heard anything about it yet.

They found a gas station nearby and got their drinks, hot chocolate and french vanilla coffee. The teenager running the register barely acknowledged them as she texted away on her cellphone. As soon as they exited, River managed to burn her tongue on her drink. She stuck her tongue out as they walked, letting the air cool it off.

Bullett asked her about the building he was looking for and she pointed down the street. As they walked they discussed cartoons between sips and River cooling her tongue. It didn't take them long to find it with River acting as a map. Bullett marveled at her, he wasn't sure if she permanently saved someone's memories or was acting on her own. If it was the former he was afraid to see how this would affect her long term.

The "house" blended in perfectly, a couple of other houses on the street looked to be in similar condition with for sale signs in the yard. He kept his head low and grabbed River's hand in case things went south. He tried to steady his pace to avoid suspicion as he scanned the street. There didn't seem to be any guards and no visible cameras though, he knew from personal experience that these could be well hidden and there were too many hiding places in the area to be completely sure they weren't being watched.

Bullett tried a new tactic, he mentally directed his thoughts to River.

"Squeeze my hand twice if you can hear me."

She squeezed twice.

"We're going to go to the end of the street and then come back, twice if you understand."

229

Twice again.

"Alright, if you sense someone else near us squeeze twice, if we're alone just one time."

She firmly gripped a single time.

"Ok, if that changes at all same thing. And if things get bad, run and don't look back. I'll be right behind you."

She looked up at him and squeezed with all her might, she knew he couldn't hear her thoughts but he picked up the message. She wasn't gonna run without him and at this point there wasn't anything he could do about it. He sighed deeply as they turned around at the intersection.

His heart began to race in a mix of fear and anticipation. He really hadn't thought of a plan yet. He figured he'd take a page from Guy's book and wing it. He looked to River to make sure she knew what he was thinking and received two squeezes in response. As they came back by the house they released hands. She stood still and watched as he sprinted towards the front door, kicking it clear off the hinges to clatter inside the main room.

He surveyed the interior while River kept an eye out for anyone approaching. The inside looked like a normal house though not an abandoned one. A couch sat in front of a tv playing an old black and white movie, pictures hung on the wall and toys scattered the floor next to a child's crib. He looked back to River who was already headed towards him.

"I think we may have the wrong house."

He continued to look around the main room, he still wasn't quite sure if this was a tactical breach or a home invasion. River caught up with him, taking his hand they both searched together.

Everything seemed lived in and dust free, an utter contrast to the house's exterior. River signaled they were alone with a single tight grip. As they circled the main room looking for any sign of something out of the ordinary, River spotted the toys on the floor. With a squeal she released his hand and dropped to the floor to play.

Bullett figured it was just as safe here as anywhere else so he was content to leave her to play.

"If anyone comes at all yell as loud as you can."

"Uh huh."

She absentmindedly nodded as she introduced a teddy bear to a car. He started to search the other rooms. More and more it started to look like he had the wrong house but something felt off, he couldn't quite put his finger on it. He made his way to a room designed for a young child. Another crib, photos, changing table, and a box full of toys all looked as normal as anything else. He turned to leave but a nagging sensation told him to take another look. He scanned the room from wall to wall several times, River could be heard giggling at some joke between her and the toys.

After a minute or two of taking in the scenery he noticed something odd. None of the pictures in this room had people in them, it was all nature scenes and artistic black and white photos. He called to the next room, fixated on the photos.

"River, do any of the pictures in there have people in them?"

"Nope!"

She called a few seconds later.

"We still good?"

"Yup! I'm still listening."

She sounded annoyed to be interrupted. Bullett felt something ominous about the pictures. What family puts up pictures without any people in them? He approached one, it was such a stock looking photo that it was almost unnoticeable. A sepia and grainy photo of a rocking chair in an empty room with a wooden floor. He lifted it from the wall, cautious of an alarm. To his surprise, behind the picture was nothing but smooth wall. His shoulders dropped in disappointment.

He knocked on parts of the wall like he'd seen in movies but wasn't quite sure what he was listening for. He ran his fingers across the paint feeling it stick, like a hand across a window, to the area behind the photo. A small square of the paint faded to black and a handprint appeared in the center. He glanced at his own hand and put it over the imprint.

A flash of red light, from behind the panel, nearly blinded him. A tiny buzz rang out from the area around his palm. Just above the door a large sheet of steel dropped down, blocking his exit. He tossed the picture to the floor and ran up to his only exit. River yelled from the other side but was muffled by the thick metal.

Bullett pressed his palms to the door and concentrated on the picture that formed in his mind. He compressed metal on the sides drawing metal away from the center. A seam formed in the center of the door forming a gap just small enough to see through. River pressed her face against the door doing her best to see through the crack.

He marveled at how quickly he was gaining control of his ability. Even though he was the one doing it, he knew he had yet to see how far he could go. Once the door had split far enough, River lunged through the opening and latched onto Bullett's leg.

"Don't leave me!"

She sobbed, still holding the teddy bear.

"You have to keep me safe!"

Bullett dropped his hands and patted her on the back.

"You're fine, I'm right here. I won't let anything happen to you."

He patted her on the back and continued to widen the gap in the metal all the while she kept her face buried in his leg. As soon as the gap was wide enough he stepped through, dragging his leg and River behind him. With large, heavy, awkward steps he made his way through a hallway. Behind him the humming of electricity pulled his attention. While he couldn't see the source of the noise, a green cloud forming on the ground indicated it was nothing good.

He dead-legged his way to the living room as quickly as he could, the fog began to overflow the child's room into the hallway. River kept her eyes shut tight, she didn't want to see whatever Bullett saw. His mind ran through the possibilities and none were good. Worse case scenario they would both die from a single breath of this tainted gas.

In the main room, the same fog poured from vents hidden under the furniture. By now, it had already wrapped around their ankles and was slowly climbing.

As he made it halfway into the room he had a thought, he turned to close the opening behind him. The gas had already risen to his knees and was rising too fast in the main room to worry about closing the hole. He hopped his way to the exit, the door here was much thicker than the first and would take longer to open.

By the time he could even see daylight he was already waist deep in the thick smoke, sweat started to form on his brow as he struggled to force the door open. He had barely opened it a few inches when the fog snaked under his peripheral, he wouldn't have enough time. He decided on brute force, gripping the inside of the small opening, he pulled at the edges like elevator doors.

Though seeping through the small gap he made, the room was filling faster than it was emptying. He took a deep breath, most likely his last one ever, and pulled with all his might. His muscles and bones strained to their limit, audibly protesting in their stretching and popping. A rattling within his shirt distracted him momentarily.

235

He had forgotten about the chain that had been so useful before. Lungs at their limit, he continued to pull as he moved the chain into the gap. He slowly split it into pillars that pushed against the door from inside the split. His chest ached from the breath he was holding. The door moved slightly, Bullett put as much effort as he could on both fronts. Finally, the door ripped like paper down the middle, a seam through the entire door.

Bullett bashed into the door, the two walls of steel indenting in the sidewalk. Once he was out of range, Bullett took a deep breath of life-affirming oxygen. He looked around, surprised to see the street empty. Looking back towards the house, he watched as swamp-like gas flowed into the yard and dissipated.

"Let's get out of here before someone notices... River?"

He looked down at his leg to find nothing but pants attached, inside the fog River lay on the floor in the doorway. Taking another deep breath, Bullett charged back in after her. Dashing back out, he carried her limp body in his arms, once out of range of the fog he placed her on the ground. He couldn't tell if she was breathing, he looked around again for any sign of life but the street remained dead as ever. He removed the bear from her hand and placed it in his bag, throwing her over his shoulder like a sleeping child he jogged down the street to find help.

Chapter 18

Wifi arrived earlier than expected. The sun had just crested over the horizon and the morning traffic was picking up into full gridlock. Wearing the same clothes from the previous day, he entered, finishing off the last of his energy drink. Shift stifled a yawn as he knocked on the connecting door to wake up Guy and went to put some hotel coffee on in the pot.

Guy drug himself through the door towards the couch. With an over exaggerated gesture he plopped down next to Wifi, who was too busy connecting his computer to notice.

"Don't you ever sleep?"

"The internet never sleeps."

Guy rested his head on the back of the couch, staring at the ceiling until Shift showed up with two fresh cups of coffee. Shift spun the chair in front of the computer desk around and stared at the near boiling caffeinated water the hotel has the nerve to call coffee. Wifi paid neither of them any attention as he finished up his normal scans and set up his proxies.

With a nod, Wifi congratulated himself on fine work as usual. He beat his previous record time by 2 seconds. With it all finally finished he could continue his purpose for being there. He spun his laptop around, a slide show already displaying on the screen. He had spent all night on it and was finally going to have the opportunity to show it off.

"Let me start by explaining what we're doing."

"Small words please." Guy spoke over the rim of his cup.

"...alright. This is the floor plan of the facility."

With the press of a button, a large 3 dimensional building rotated into view before becoming transparent. The camera rotated to a top view and had several points highlighted in several colors. Wifi smiled inside, knowing they would be impressed at his handy work. Neither Shift nor Guy noticed the computer. Guy was busing counting Wifi's words to see if it worked like sheep while Shift contemplated burning down the manufacturing plant of the most awful coffee he had ever had.

"If you'll notice here, there is a small security panel. If you can disable... break it, you won't have to worry about alarms."

Guy reached over and shut the laptop, 32 words and he was still awake.

"Wifi, Wifi I need you to look at me and stop talking."

Wifi was a bit taken aback, no one ever physically messed with his equipment. He looked to Guy much like a child kicked in the testicles for the first time.

"Wifi, it's early. Just give us an address and we'll go do this real quick so we can come back and sleep. This 6 AM shit is for the birds."

Shift nodded, not in agreement but in nearly planting his nose in the warm cup. He jumped slightly, looking around to see if anyone noticed he had fallen asleep.

With a sigh, Wifi handed Guy a cleverly crafted business card he had made himself. He took special care to ensure the weight and print were perfectly matched to those the company used themselves.

"The address on that is accurate but the rest is all an alias just in case you get caught with it."

Guy ripped the card in half, saving just the address section for safe keeping in his pocket.

Wifi closed his eyes and took a deep breath. "I despise you both. Now get on with it before I tell them you're coming."

Guy went back to his room to get changed. He returned to Shift lying face first on the couch snoring, Wifi had already packed and left. Guy grabbed the relay from the table before he kicked at Shift to wake him.

"Hey! Let's go."

Shift rolled to feet, oblivious to the world as they stumbled to the door. They made their way to the lobby and into the morning sunlight. Squinting against the light pointed directly at them, Guy pulled out the scrap of paper with the address on it. He cursed under his breath at Wifi, it was several miles away.

The two arrived at the location just before eight, employee cars were already parked in the large parking lot. The two had managed to wake up on their hike after Shift nearly stumbled into traffic. The facility in front of them was larger than expected. Three buildings all stood inside a several acre plant lined with chain link fence.

Guy studied the paper, it didn't say which building they needed to place the device in.

"Ugh... how are we supposed to know-"

"That one." Shift pointed to the building on the right.

"How do you know?"

"It says "Central" on the wall. Pretty obvious right?"

"Well then Sherlock… after you."

They circled around the right of everything, approaching the fence from a blind spot. Shift kept an eye out for cameras while Guy vaulted over and sprinted next to the wall. He motioned for Shift to follow and soon the two were standing in front of the entrance door.

Shift tried the knob, of course it was locked. He closed his eyes for a second then pushed at the door, leaving the metal catch in the frame. A long hallway lay before them, lights dimmed indicating no one was inside. Still, to be careful the two crouched and went door to door looking for something that looked "computery" as Shift put it.

They turned the corner and continued searching rooms until the lights in the building all lit up at once. Guy put a hand into Shift's back, shoving him into the room in front of him. Down the hall the voices of employees echoed off the walls, indicating their approach. There was no telling how long they'd have to find the room.

The room was mainly bare, no windows or even vents. Just a computer desk with a computer, filing cabinet, potted plant, and a small trash can in the corner.

Guy yell/whispered to Shift. "What do we do?"

242

Responding in kind. "I don't know, you're the one with the thingy."

"This is no time to talk about my penis."

"I meant the relay thing."

"Oh, well here." He handed the box to Shift. "Hide it somewhere."

"Where?"

"I don't know, somewhere they won't find it. We should be close enough for it to still work."

Shift quickly looked around for a good hiding spot. Footsteps were approaching. The decorative plant? No, that would be discarded at some point. The inside of the computer? Same problem. He finally hit a stroke of genius. He dashed to an inner wall and phased his hand and the device through it. He let it go inside, hearing it thud on the ground inside the wall.

He turned to Guy with a thumbs up. Guy put a finger to his lips just as two people walked passed the door, engrossed in a conversation pitting ninjas versus pirates. Cracking the door slightly he surveyed the hall. As far as he could tell it was empty, but who knew for how long. He motioned for Shift to follow and ducked out of the room, continuing down the hall. Hopefully, they would be able to find an alternate exit.

They rounded another corner, hoping to circle back to the entrance only to come to a dead end. Another locked door, Shift opened it the same as before and they both entered. Inside was a massive server room, temperature controlled and humming. Guy cast a disapproving look towards Shift.

"If you still had it we could have put it here…. dumbass."

"You said to hide it!"

"Well, that's what you get for being a follower."

"Let's just look for a way out of here."

The two searched the room bottom to top before Guy spotted a maintenance hatch in the far corner of the ceiling. They had a way out but no way to reach it, there wasn't a ladder attached.

Behind them the door shut, indicating someone entered the room. Guy and Shift simultaneously look to each other for the next move. There were rows of servers in the way so they still had a few precious seconds before being caught.

"Get on my shoulders." Guy whispered, dropping to a kneel.

Shift didn't argue, he almost jumped onto Guy in his hurry. Standing like a human ladder they were still several feet short of reaching any kind of hold. Guy jumped, in his apex Shift jumped as well. His fingers grazed the bottom of the only bar available before they both crashed to the floor.

"Hey! Who's there?" A voice nervously called from the other side of the room.

"I have a plan." Guy whispered.

A very skinny man in thick glasses searched between servers looking for the noise. He zigzagged his way from one side of the room to the other, this wouldn't be the first time someone had snuck in to move wires around so they got better speeds in the office. But he wasn't about to get written up for not catching them this time. He made his way to the back of the room, but over the humming radiating out from every corner of the room he couldn't hear much.

He approached the corner of the room, inspecting the latch leading to the roof. It looked untouched, there used to be a lock there before one of the air conditioning repair guys stole it. This wasn't the time to dwell on such things. He shrugged, maybe it was just one of the coolant systems kicking on. He would need to make a report about it. He turned to leave when something caught his attention in his peripheral.

Rounding the corner, Guy and Shift had resumed their human ladder. They circled one of the servers leaning forward slightly using Shift as a counter balance. The man barely had time to react, jumping backwards in his shock.

With a slight crouch, Guy leapt forward towards the man. A foot planted onto his shoulder locking him in place as Guy launched upwards. Shift jumped higher and firmly grasped the bar with one hand while simultaneously reaching up to open the hatch. Guy dropped onto the floor along with the other man. As the man slowly got to his feet Guy jumped off of his back up to Shift's leg. He grabbed onto Shift and swung himself through the opening. He threw his arm back through the hatch, gripping Shift around the wrist and lifting him onto the roof with him.

Below, the man ran out of the room, yelling for security. They both looked to each other and laughed as they ran to the edge of the roof, jumped to the ground and hopped the fence. Invigorated, they decided to take the scenic route home to burn off their extra energy.

Guy felt a vibrating in his pocket. Reaching in, he grabbed the headset Wifi had given him.

246

"Hello?"

"Good work gentlemen, it looks like I'm in. The signal isn't at one hundred percent but it'll definitely function for what I require. Return home, I have a bit of digging to do. I'll contact y'all when it's completed."

Chapter 19

Bullett gently rocked back and forth, the sound of the wheels on the track a gentle lullaby. He sat dangling a leg through the opening hatch beneath him. He breathed in deep, enjoying the smell of the fall leaves as the train treked it's way across the state. The morning sun gently caressing the grass as it peeked over the distant hills.

He wondered how long it would be before they arrived, the train stopped every so often for reasons he could only guess at. Every now and then someone would go car to car checking for hitchhikers and maintenance issues, he learned a few tricks to avoid detection the from the self proclaimed "vagabonds" he'd met before. The easiest of which was to jam the door closed, they were fond of using a stick whereas he could simply bond the metal together.

He smirked to himself, in all of the places in the world, who would ever expect to find someone with superpowers hiding in the cargo on a train. The train lurched forwards, a tale-tale sign they were stopping for another check. Bullett grabbed the door to the hatch and jumped inside onto the stacks of hay. Luckily they were piled high enough for him to reach the hatch from inside. He quickly sealed the lock to the frame and found a spot to sit.

"Bullett?"

A groggy voice called from the darkness.

"Over here River."

Bullett called back patting the wall next to him. The light shining through the holes drilled into the top of the railroad car cast heavy shadows between the rays. Even in the difficult lighting, Bullett could clearly see River was still wrapped in the blanket he had draped over her.

"Wh..where are we?"

"On a train, headed to Austin. We're going to meet a friend of mine."

He knew it was useless to lie to her even in this state. He'd prefer to ignore the truth and have her go back to sleep but that wouldn't work with her.

"Are we going to see Guy?"

"Mmhmm, we'll be a little early but that gives us time to find him."
She nodded and rubbed her eyes.

"Can we go to the park when we get there?"

"Sure, we'll try to find a really big one to play in."

She struggled to her feet, grabbing the blanket and bear Bullet had placed next to her and staggered her way towards him. She plopped down next to him and curled up, nuzzling the stuffed animal.

"Thank you," She yawned. "you're a good big brother."

Whether she was teasing him or not, it still tugged on his heart.

"And you're a good little sister."

He patted her head and closed his eyes as he rested his head on the bale of hay behind him. The train slowly started moving again, jerking a few times before finding a rhythm. The two were rocked to sleep to the soft swaying of the locomotive.

Bullett awoke the next time the train sputtered to a stop. Surprisingly, he felt well rested. He hadn't really thought about it until now but, he needed less and less sleep to feel fully rested. He looked down at the drooling River, still peacefully asleep with her bear gripped under an arm. It was good she was sleeping comfortably, comfort was going to be increasingly difficult to come by.

He waited for the train to move again before he climbed back out of the top hatch. He decided to do a bit of training while he had the opportunity. With a bit of concentration, he managed to push metal from underneath his skin. Looking closely he noticed a trickle of blood coating the metal. Leaving it attached to the skin, he shaped it into various shapes. The more he shaped it the faster he got.

At first he just made basic shapes from cubes to triangles to spheres, he then moved on to more complex shapes. Anything he could imagine he was able to form out of metal, animals, miniature people, even landscapes. Eventually he moved to weapons, blades and hammer-heads mostly. With time he was able to start making moving objects, his first being a butterfly knife. He detached the knife from his skin and flipped it around, feeling the movement and flow against itself.

Time passed as he became more proficient in his power, it was during a practice with using both hands to shape at the same time that he saw the sign indicating Austin city limits. He quickly absorbed the metal again and jumped into the train car to wake up River. They would need to exit before too long to avoid detection.

Not yet fully awake, River held on to Bullett's back as he jumped from the slowing train. They slid to a stop in the gravel next to the tracks, watching the train come to a stop further down the track. Bullett bent down, allowing River to stand on her own feet and stuffed the rest of the blanket back into his pack. She rubbed a sleepy eye as she reached for his hand.

"Where are we going now?"

"I dunno, let's go explore until we find something interesting."

She half-nodded, holding back a yawn as they headed down the nearest street. Walking in the shadows of towering buildings they aimlessly observed their surroundings. Austin was a totally different city from Dallas, everything felt so alive and vibrant. It would be easy to get lost in this city, a pair of snowflakes drifting in a blizzard. Bullett marveled at the environment, he'd never been here before but everything felt like home. The city seemed to fit into the environment like a puzzle piece, the trees, the people, the waters and stone, all becoming one glowing picture.

Large crowds of people poured from the nearby train into the already overflowing street. Hordes of fans flooded the streets in preparation for a football game. Further down the street people grilled different types of meat from the back of their trucks. Almost everyone wore jerseys and quite a few had face paint on to match. Bullett already knew this indicated a sports match would be happening soon and by extension so did River.

River's face lit up with excitement, while she was being bombarded with all the thoughts around her, she was able to gleam the electric feel of it all and wanted to see the game herself. She squeezed Bullett's hand looking up at him with big doe eyes.

"Can we go?" She pleaded.

"I don't see why not, as long as they let us in."

Bullett decided there was no harm in it, they wouldn't really lose out on more than a few hours and they'd get to have a little fun. Besides, with as many people as there were around, there was a chance (however small) they'd run into Guy.

River raised a fist and cheered like a few of the passerbys she had seen. As they worked their way through the mass of people they were greeted like fellow fans. Everyone behaved as family, they were offered burgers and drinks which they gladly accepted. River got to have her face painted like an orange kitten and given a giant lollipop for being so good at sitting still.

Beaming from ear to ear, River skipped along as they followed the flow of pedestrians for several miles towards a nearby campus. Towering above them, a clock tower was lit up in all orange from various lights. Near the base, people of all ages gathered in preparation for the big event. Bullett glanced at the clock which indicated just after noon. He asked a nearby guy speaking loudly to his fans what time the game started, after a few jabs at the validity of his fandom they informed him they still had hours to go.

River was a bit sad she would have to wait but was no less excited to be included in the frenzy. She saw another girl her age and waved, the girl softly waved back. Even though River didn't know her she wanted to make a new friend. She dragged Bullett towards the other girl and immediately introduced herself. Bullett was thrust into awkward conversation with the girl's father as the two girls spoke.

Minutes went by with Bullett doing his best to scrape by with any sport related knowledge he possessed. River found her conversation just as troublesome, the other girl was less receptive to being interrupted than Bullett. Eventually both groups fell flat in conversation, it was mid sentence that he noticed the crowd around him had all started gasping and pointing to an area behind him.

Turning, he noticed the clock tower looked different. Windows were slightly askew, uneven sections of concrete were now crumbling dirt, and the upper floors seemed to emanate their own maroon tinted light.

"It's a damn prank."

The man Bullett had been engaged with shouted exasperated as he slapped his hat across his thigh in apparent anger. Many more shouts came from all around as a long booing erupted.

"There! In the window!"

Returning his hat to his head, the man pointed along with several others. Tensions rose as more of the building began to shine and shift.

"How are they doing that?"

He put a hand on Bullett's shoulder, shaking him as though to rile him up as well.

"Some good 'ole fashion Texas justice should put them in their place."

The crowd had already begun to press forward as people charged into the building. Bullett felt his stomach drop, none of this seemed right. This wasn't just an illusion or trick, something was seriously wrong.

Many more windows suddenly shifted different directions, making the tower look like a Picasso painting. River shouted in anger with the rest of the crowd, not fully understanding the weight of what was happening. Bullett was shoved to the side as the man pushed past him, daughter lifted onto his shoulders. Grabbing him by the elbow Bullett turned the man towards him.

"This isn't right, something is terribly wrong."

People poured into the tower, climbing stairs and searching room by room. Outside cracks ripped through the walls originating from the glowing spots. Bullett grabbed River's hand and tried to push his way past the forming mob. The wall of people paid him no attention as they pressed forward still shouting and booing. Glancing back at the tower the only thing not glowing was the clock face itself, hands still frozen at 12:05. Bullett wasn't going to wait for the outcome, he pulled River up and tucked her under his arm like a football.

Forcing his way through the crowd, he used his superior strength to toss obstacles out of his way as easily as running through inflatable tubes, hairs raised on the back of his neck, River protested in vain, her struggles getting her nowhere. Leaving a trail of angry people on the ground, he continued his path away from the tower.

Above the angry shouts, blaring music and charging mob Bullett heard the distinct sound of shattering glass. He turned briefly to see someone falling from a fourth floor window. As the body disappeared behind the onlookers, a crack formed through the whole building from one corner to another, forming a lightning strike in the brick and mortar. A shockwave erupted out of the crack throwing the closest to the source into the air like rag dolls. Before it reached its apex, a wall of white flame spewed forth with white hot intensity, those unlucky to be at the forefront of the diagonal flame were set ablaze in screaming agony.

The mob scattered every direction, their fear louder than their screams. Bullett continued to mow his way through the mob, no longer able to make a scene he sprinted as fast as he could, melting like a shadow in the chaos. The fire passed over the two with a thunderous boom, leaving a suffocating heat in it's wake.

The tower, unable to take the strain any longer, began to collapse under it's own weight. The shimmering stone throwing sparks and flames as it scraped against itself. Dust bellowed from the shattering windows, coating the ground in a growing darkness. Bullett had already worked his way towards the back of the crowds. Emerging onto the streets, he continued to run, jumping over cars and pedestrians alike in an effort to put as much distance as possible between them and the tower.

In the distance a loud crack burst forth, rippling through the surrounding area for miles. Before the echos dissipated an explosion erupted from the epicenter of the collapsing building, immediately cratering the site and overwhelming the neighboring buildings which fell like dominos. The combination of ash, cinders, and dirt swept for miles.

257

Bullett turned at the explosion and watched as the volcano-like eruption killed dozens. As the thickening cloud of refuse approached he sat River down and used his own body to shield her. They, and miles of innocent people, vanished amidst the dust and flames. River held tightly to Bullett as he yelled to hold her breath, struggling to balance against the rushing surge of wind.

A shadow dashed through the chaos gripping Bullett on the shoulder.

"Follow me."

The man's voice stood out against the swirling dust storm. A hand grabbed Bullett's wrist and pulled him lightly. There was nothing menacing in his words and seeing as how he didn't have a better plan, Bullett complied. He lifted River around to his back allowing her to hang on and moved with him.

Almost completely blinded, he couldn't tell which direction they were headed. They turned several times and stopped every now and then when Bullett stumbled. Covered in ash and dirt they finally walked through a door, the sounds of chaos still echoing behind them.

A storage room greeted them, concrete walls and a tin roof made it feel more like a bunker. Shelves lined the side walls with a platform ahead with a door leading further in. The man leading them continued ahead, climbing the stairs and walking onto the platform as though it was his personal stage.

"At last we meet!"

He exclaimed, arms raised towards them in greeting. Bullett shut the door and let River down, they both wiped the dirt from as much of them as possible. Bullett turned to the man as he continued to dust himself off.

"Thanks for that, not to be rude but... who are you?"

The man paused and looked around as though surveying his audience. Looking back to his rescued pair he cocked his head like a confused animal.

"That's... hmm, lemme see. At this point I believe you'll call me Gl.. no wait, Mod. Yes, Mod is my name to you. This is the first time we've met yeah?"

Bullett looked to River, unsure as to the sanity of the man.

Can you read anything from this guy?

She visibly strained, squinting her eyes at him while he patiently waited for a response. She looked back to Bullett and shook her head no. That alone was enough to worry Bullett. He decided to play it by ear.

"No, I can't say we have. Why did you help us?"

"First time meeting, let me think a sec. You've skipped a few steps, or maybe I just have them backwards. It's so hard to tell lately, I've become a bit of a mess. Let's see... you've already left Dallas, did you just arrive in Austin today?"

Bullett stepped in front of River.

"Have you been following us? Who are you and what do you want from us?"

Mod mumbled something to himself before responding.

"Following you? No, this is the first time I've seen you with my own eyes. However, you're very well known. As for what I want... well, I just want you to be where you're supposed to be."

"What does that even mean?"

Bullett was getting frustrated, he had already started forming a blade in his sleeve just in case.

"I don't really have a way that I can put it without spoiling anything and we all hate spoilers."

"Well then... what's the plan?"

Mod clapped his hands, bouncing excitedly.

"You're exactly as I'd heard! Maybe still a little green but straight to the point, I love it! There's a credit card and a piece of paper on the shelf beside you, the paper has an address and time written down. Take them both and don't be late."

"Late for what? I'm not taking anything until I know what's going on."

Mod held up his finger like a teacher silencing the room and tilted his head, listening behind him. After a few seconds he continued their conversation.

"The key word is Shift... no wait, Guy. That's a silly name.. well I guess to people like Mod and Bullett, it fits right in. I hate spoilers but I really want to see what happens for myself. Guy will be there, be on your guard. And that card will last until you don't need it anymore."

Bullett relaxed slightly, the man may be crazy but if he wanted to kill them he wouldn't offer them money before hand.

"So what, you can see the future or something? I've got to say, after all I've seen in the past few months it honestly wouldn't surprise me."

"Or something would be more accurate. Don't worry about it for now, it'll only confuse you. I'll show up in a later chapter in your life and we can discuss it then. For now, I suggest taking the items and going. You've got a really difficult time ahead and you want to be well prepared. If not, you *will* die."

He put heavy emphasis on the "will", as though it were fact. Not waiting for a response he smiled and gave a quick bow before exiting through the door behind him. No words, no advice, he just left the two in dumfounded silence.

Bullett looked to River.

"You get anything at all from him?"

"Nu uh, it was like a bunch of people were all talking at once. It hurt my head to try and listen to him."

Bullett nodded almost to himself, this Mod guy was an interesting character to say the least. But he knew Guy somehow, either they were going to somehow meet up with Guy or walk straight into a trap. They didn't really have any other leads either way.

Bullett grabbed the paper and card to examine them. The card didn't have a name on it, just a very fancy looking business credit card. The paper gave directions from a hotel to a downtown address but it didn't have a date. Bullett palmed his forehead, he had to be crazy to trust this guy.

A siren passed by outside reminding him of recent events. It would be best if they weren't directly involved in anything further. He decided to look for the hotel listed on the note. The least he could do is find his starting point. River tugged at his sleeve beaming from ear to ear.

"He said endless ice cream right?"

"No, he said we'd have enough money to survive for a while."

"I can't survive without ice cream!"

She giggled, she was already learning to use her powers to her advantage. She knew with certainty which strings she could pull to get her way. She could become very dangerous one day. Hopefully the world's ice cream supply would last until then. Bullett sighed in defeat.

"Can we at least find this hotel first?"

"Yes sir." She said in her best soldier voice with a salute. Bullett cracked the door, scanning the street before motioning for her to follow him. She stiffly marched behind him onto the ash covered street. Oblivious to the death and destruction as they looked for the hotel.

Chapter 20

Shift and Guy worked their way through the streets both beaming. As they passed through a park, Guy felt the communicator vibrate in his ear.

"Can y'all hear me? This is urgent!"

"Woah woah, I'm here Wifi. What's going on?"

"After my relay was set up and running, I started doing a little bit of digging in various places. Suddenly the net went haywire with information. I'm not exactly sure on the details yet but all I know is you were specifically mentioned and someone with the alias Bullett. Is that someone you know?"

Guy stopped in his tracks, with everything happening so quickly he had forgotten all about Bullett. How could he forget about someone that helped him claw out of hell? Shift stood and watched, Guy's expression conveyed more than enough for him to understand the gravity of the situation.

"What exactly are they saying?" Guy's voice wavered, he feared the worse.

"I don't know the exact situation but there's a location they're converging on and I believe he's there. I'll forward it to your phone."

Guy whipped his phone from his back pocket, the screen lit up with an incoming message. He tapped at it, bringing up a gps location directing him a few miles away. Looking to Shift, he nodded and started running in the direction it gave him. Shift followed closely behind not sure what else to do.

"Wifi, I'm gonna need more details."

"Already working on it, it looks like this isn't just one group. I'm showing multiple government agencies working together with an unknown organization, give me a moment."

Shift pipped up. "What's going on here Guy?"

"Remember the guy that I was telling you about that escaped with me?"

"Yeah, isn't he in Dallas?"

"Turns out he's in Austin, not far from here and he's in trouble."

Shift ran up shoulder to shoulder with him, a worried expression on his face.

"How much trouble?"

"From what it sounds like, a metric boat load."

"Guy, I don't really know this other guy or anything but, should we really be putting ourselves at risk to save him? I mean, we were barely able to handle that nazi chick. Wouldn't it be safer to let him get himself out?"

"Yep."

"But we're going anyways?"

"Yep."

"Got a plan?"

"None whatsoever."

Shift laughed. "Alright, but i'm letting you know now. If things get too dicey I'm out."

Guy's bluetooth crackled in his ear, Wifi spoke in a mixture of amazement and fear.

"So this other entity... It's Holy. I don't know how but Holy is commanding multiple government agencies from the FBI down to the local police. This is above my paygrade. I've gotta burn and relocate. I'll contact you when I'm sure it's safe."

"Wait! Wifi!"

The crackle followed by static told them they were on their own for the time being. He put the communicator back in his pocket. They were running into the thick of chaos, and they would be going in blind.

~-~-~-~-~

Bullett slid a freshly made knife into his sleeve, attaching it to the skin on his wrist. He kept his back to the brick wall while scanning the street. The address he had been given put them in front of a massive bank, complete with an enclosed parking garage. He and River arrived early to scan for an ambush. He still wasn't sure he trusted Mod but, at least he gave them enough money for a room for the night so they could clean up.

A car drove up to the entrance of the parking garage just around the corner of the two. He watched as the swinging arm rose to allow it inside. As soon as it disappeared up the ramp he tugged at River's wrist, pulling her with him inside.

Sticking to the wall, doing their best to stay in the shadows of the dimly lit garage, they inched forward into the depths of the brick and mortar box. The echoing of footsteps stopped them in their tracks. Ducking low Bullett carefully surveyed the whole floor for the source. Ahead, a woman in a business dress and heels walked towards the entrance to the building.

With a sigh of relief they continued forward. Seeing nothing of note they moved to the second floor, following the car ramp rather than taking the stairs. After searching the second level for a while, they moved on to the third floor. This one stood out from the others. Only a few cars dotted the area, cautiously they continued their search.

Near a pillar towards the back end of the garage River noticed a note, taped to the pillar itself with "Bullett" written in pink highlighter on the front. Bullett snatched it down and quickly read it. Sprawled inside was a short message written in the same pink ink.

Bullett,
If you've got the time to read this then I was right. Based on your previous interactions I guessed you'd show up early to check for bombs or something. The time I gave you was an hour later than you needed to be here. If you showed up early then things are going to get interesting real soon.

With love and respect,
Mod

Bullett crumpled the paper and threw it to the ground. Taking the knife from his sleeve he handed it to River.

"Hide that, if anyone tries to hurt you don't be afraid to use it."

"Who's gonna hurt me?"

She was starting to get worried, Bullett's mind was trying to calculate for every possibility. All the while River was trying to keep up. She could only retain bits and pieces, leaving her worried and confused. Bullett knelt down in front of her, petting her on the head like a child.

"No one if I can help it."

He forced a smile and took her hand. Though he knew it was pointless to lie to her, he was doing it more for himself. Everything about this situation felt wrong, hopefully with a smile and some courage he'd be able to get them both out. Across the garage he spotted another door leading into the bank. He decided to work his way through the bank to get out. Hopefully there'd be enough people for them to blend in with.

~-~-~-~-~

Guy and Shift stopped in front of a towering bank, the almost 30 story tall building looming over them with steel and tinted glass. Guy double checked his phone.

"This is the location Wifi sent."

"We can't search floor by floor, that'll take forever!"

"Well the top floors are probably all CEOs and such, so that'll take a few off. I figure we just take it one at a time. Thirty minutes tops."

"You said people were on their way though."

"So we take the stairs then, that'll cut out some time."

Without giving him a chance to come up with another argument, Guy walked through the doors into the lobby area. With an exasperated sigh, Shift followed behind him. Inside was larger than either expected. The main room was several floors tall. An elaborate chandelier hung from the overly victorian ceiling giving off a faux natural light.

People clamored everywhere, most in business suits or high dollar clothing. The two men stuck out like sore thumbs, getting more than a few stares working their way through the lobby. Guy had to resist the urge to make a scene, he was prone to making people uncomfortable for the fun of it but this wasn't the time.

"Maybe he's somewhere in the lobby?"

Shift pointed towards a pathway overlooking the lobby. "There's a bunch of offices and stuff up there, and a bird's eye view couldn't hurt."

"Fair point."

They both headed towards the stairs leading above the lobby when a uniformed security guard stepped in front of them.

"Can I help you?"

The aging guard spoke in a cold manner, he already had his mind set on kicking them out. Guy responded quickly. "Yes sir, you see my partner and I were out and about when we were mugged. I need to close my business account immediately before our funds are lost to some hooligans."

The guard didn't buy it, he pointed towards the door and grabbed Shift by the arm. "Alright you two, time to go."

He gripped Shift tightly, lifting up on the shoulder while grabbing the back of Guy's shirt and pushing them both towards the door. Guy looked to Shift for some help. He shrugged, their on-the-fly plan failed and they had no back up. Guy took a deep breath, exhaling slowly.

"Well, I tried. Sorry but we don't have time for this."

Guy threw his elbow up into the man's nose, shattering it on impact. Instinctively he released his grip on both men to cup his injured face. Shift turned and threw a knee into his stomach before running past him. Guy grabbed the guard's shirt and threw him to the floor before running after Shift.

The scene was less than stealthy, having already drawn attention to themselves, their attack elicited screams from someone nearby as the lobby went into chaos. One of the clerks hit a panic button and the patrons scattered towards the door. This actually proved to be advantageous to the duo as it provided enough cover to make it hard to track where they went.

~-~-~-~-~

Bullett and River entered into a large open office area. Phones rang and people buzzed about conducting business. Bullett noticed a sign pointing to the elevator on the other side of the room past all the cubicles. They made their way to the back wall, Bullett tried to pull her behind him discretely. A woman stepped out of a cubicle without notice, bumping directly into them.

"Oh excuse me I wasn't looking… um, who are you?"

She raised an eyebrow glancing from him to River and back. Bullett gave a quick glance to see if anyone else noticed and lowered his voice.

"Please don't tell anyone we're here. Listen, I'm the I.T. guy and I don't have a babysitter. We were just on our way out. Please don't get me fired, I'm all she has."

He pulled River in front of him, hoping she was giving puppy eyes like he was. River was already ahead of him. Wide eyed she made her lip quiver a bit, a trick she learned worked well on adults.

"Please don't make my daddy lose his job."

The woman put a hand to her mouth. "Aww, I won't do that sweetie. You have a wonderful dad who does works hard and makes us all proud. I won't say anything I promise. Oh! Before you go.."

She went back to her desk quickly and returned with a lollipop in hand. She bent to eye level with River handing her the treat. "This is for you sweetie, I hope you like blueberry."

"I do!" River said almost too loudly as she excitedly unwrapped the candy.

"That's for being such a good girl while your daddy works."

She patted her on the head and stood back up facing Bullett. "And this is for you."

She handed him a scrap of paper with a number written on it. She smiled, tucking her hair behind her ear.

"You are such a good father... you should call me sometime."

Bullett's face noticeably reddened.

"Uh, um, thank you. We, uh.. should really go."

She giggled and looked to River.

"Hope to see you again sweetie."

River nodded excitedly, enjoying the candy as Bullett pulled her towards the elevator. She waved goodbye trying not to trip as Bullett tugged her along. They reached the elevator quickly and quietly, he spammed the button praying one of the two elevators would get there fast. Their situation went from dire to awkward and he wasn't sure how to handle it.

The doors opened, luckily it was empty. Stepping in Bullett hit the first floor button and spammed the door close, again praying to the elevator god. As they started shutting, the elevator next to them opened. A lady came running out screaming.

"The bank's being robbed!"

Bullett reached to stop the doors but it was too late, they shut before he could hear the rest. They started descending to the first floor, giving him little time to prepare. He slapped a hand to the metal rail and started absorbing as much metal as he could. River didn't have a care in the world as long as she had her candy.

~-~-~-~-~

Shift stomped up the stairs in anger with Guy on his heels.

"Oh! It'll be easy! We'll just walk right in and start beating up people! Way to be super obvious." Shift scolded Guy, though both knew they didn't really have an option.

"Hey, you're the one that put a knee in his bowels."

"After you broke his nose!"

"Well... we all make mistakes. Speaking of, where are we?"

"I don't know, I was just trying to get out of there. Third or fourth floor I think."

They swung open the nearest door into an office-type area. Across the room a lady came running out of an elevator.

"The bank's being robbed!"

Shift looked to Guy and gestured towards the woman.

"See what you did?"

"Fine... I'm sorry, happy?"

"Not particularly, let's get out of here before you nuke the place."

"One sec, I can fix this."

Guy jumped onto the nearest table, holding his hands up. "Excuse me ladies and gentlemen, can I have your attention please. I would just like to inform you all than we are not, in fact, robbing the bank."

He looked towards the woman that caused the commotion, only to be met with a look of confusion. She burst out in anger.

"Of course YOU aren't robbing the bank, dozens of men in masks with guns just made their way to the second floor. They're demanding specific transfers to other banks. They could be here any second."

Guy stood perplexed, he looked to Shift who shrugged and pointed down. Guy hopped off the table and they both entered back into the stairwell to head downstairs. As soon as they shut the door behind them a woman came sprinting up the stairs.

"Please! Somebody he-"

A bullet ripped through her skull, splattering the wall beside her as she collapsed to the floor. Both men dropped to a crouch and approached the railing. Shift peered over the top quickly and dropped back down.

"She wasn't lying, there's like 3 guys in masks with guns. What do we do?"

Shift's past experiences told him to get out, but he was down the rabbit hole and Guy was his only guide.

"I'm pretty sure whatever is going on has to do with Bullett, if we can take these guys out we may be able to find him."

"Alright then, first thing's first. We need weapons."

Guy stood to his feet and looked over the rail at the men guarding the floor below. He smirked to himself, they were grouped together. Clearly amateurs in tactics.

"Simple enough, let's take theirs."

With that he hopped over the edge, planting a knee into the closest man's back. In the same motion, he rolled forward and punched a second in his lower ribs. With a loud crack the man crumpled under the pain of his broken bones. Guy grabbed his pistol before he hit the ground and fired two shots, taking out the remaining men.

Shift hopped down next to one of the dead men. Doing his best not to look him in the eye as he wrestled the semi-automatic rifle from him. Slinging it over his shoulder, he grabbed a pistol from another man while Guy retrieved spare clips for them both.

Once both had armed themselves as well as they could they approached the door. Shift phased the lock so they could silently open the door. Peeking inside there were dozens of men walking around in masks, some holding guns to people lying on the ground and others yelling at people working on computers. The men inside were heavily armed and armored. Some wore bullet-proof vests and carried fully-automatic weapons, Guy swore he saw someone with a grenade launcher in the back.

With a sigh Shift patted Guy on the shoulder. "It was short but it was fun."

Guy smiled and shook his hand. "Last to die wins."

They threw open the door, firing before they were noticed. It didn't take long for the bullets to start flying. Guy jumped from table to table, spinning in the air as he shot. Shift dashed through the oncoming rain of bullets, pausing behind cover every now and then to solidify. Taking cover, he reloaded then jumped up to pop off another shot. As soon as he appeared from his hiding spot, a bullet ripped through his shoulder.

Guy landed in front of one of the men and headbutted him in the face before spinning him around and grabbing the back of his jacket. He ran forward, using the guy as a bullet sponge as he made his way towards the back of the room. He slid to a stop when he saw the grenade launcher being aimed in his direction. Using his human shield, he jumped off the man's back just before impact. The floor collapsed, dropping bodies and debris below.

Guy glanced down the hole into the lobby, with a nod he turned and threw his gun at the man with the launcher. Bursting into a full sprint, Guy slid under a desk and hopped over another landing face-to-face with the man. Using a leg sweep and an elbow he quickly knocked the man out. The glass panels began to shatter and fall to the street below as bullets flew everywhere. Outside a helicopter slowly lowered towards them.

~-~-~-~-~

The doors to the elevator opened allowing Bullett and River to step out. As soon as they stepped foot into the lobby Bullett cursed his luck. Cops stood with guns drawn on multiple men in masks in a stand-off. Outside sirens wailed in approach, several large, plain white vans pulled up and men clad in SWAT gear poured out. The cops and robbers yelled demands back and forth, neither lowering their weapons.

With glass shattering, the SWAT teams breached through every available opening. They paused seeing the display before them as though it was unexpected. Without warning, they started shooting each masked man in an unbiased exchange of fire. Civilian and criminal alike went down in the bloody battle.

Bullett covered River and moved towards the exit, his only thought was getting her out alive. As they neared the broken glass another team in riot gear entered and dove towards them both, using the shields to push them back against the wall. Bullett tried to protest. Backs against the wall he held his hands up in surrender, still standing in front of River.

With the criminals in the lobby dead, all guns pointed towards him. Again, he tried to speak and was shot directly in the forehead. The blood pulsed through his body and River screamed in his mind. A mixture of anger and self preservation swelled inside him. Knowing full well he was outmanned and outgunned he fought back.

A katana sliding from his sleeve, he drove the blade over the top of a shield into a man's throat. As his lifeless body dropped Bullett spun the shield around and used it to deflect bullets as he continued. Keeping River behind him, he did what he could to force his body to absorb the bullets rather than let them pass through him. It was starting to become a switch now, he didn't need to concentrate as much to get it to work right.

Taking out another shielded man, Bullett jumped backwards and handed River the first to hold in front of herself, then he scooped the second from the floor and threw it with all his might into the group of men. Using the small gap he created, Bullett dove into the middle of them to continue fighting. Grabbing one man's face, a familiar chain-like snake slid down his arm and lashed like a whip at others nearby while Bullett slammed the man into the ground.

Bullett swung wildly with his sword and chain, doing what he could to keep them at bay. Suddenly the roof above them exploded, bringing the chandelier down onto several cops. Glancing up to the new damage, Bullett briefly made eye-contact with a familiar face. Guy was looking down the hole directly at him. With a nod, Bullett promised to himself to make it out alive to see him again. Guy nodded back and threw a gun out of sight. He was in his own fight and couldn't assist right now.

A renewed sense of self washed over Bullett, he had been acting on instinct the whole time. What was the point of practicing every day if he wasn't going to use his various skills? In a swift motion, Bullett attached the back of the chain to the bottom of his sword. He kicked at the chain dragging the ground, mentally directing it towards a SWAT member. As it barely missed him, Bullett jerked the sword in the opposite direction stabbing a man. The momentum of his sword carried into the snake which sunk it's teeth into the SWAT member's clothing, dragging him to the ground.

As the man slid to Bullet's feet he sunk the sword into his back, the stinging of gunfire almost unnoticed. He glanced around, seeing the fear in their eyes. Several had stopped firing and a few even stepped to the back of the circle around him. He would win this fight, he had to. A man charged forward, knife in hand, sinking it into Bullett's abdomen. Without thinking, Bullett had his hand around the man's throat squeezing the life from him. Another cop tried pulling the man away by the ankle but Bullett stood firm, looking the man in the eyes while his life was fading.

"Bullett!"

River's scream snapped him out of his bloodlust. Towards the entrance a man had repelled from a helicopter and grabbed River. They were both being lifted into the air, already out of jumping height. Gathering up his chain, Bullett plowed through the men and sprinted towards the exit. Just before making it out, he threw the snake into the solid section of wall above the window.

In full sprint, he disconnected the sword and wrapped the remaining chain around his wrist. He jumped just before the chain became taught, using momentum to carry him upwards towards River. As he reached the apex of his swing he realized he was too short. He wouldn't be able to reach her.

They ascended above him in slow motion, River reaching for him and screaming yet he was helpless. He turned to the building to see Guy running towards him but too far away to help. He looked back up to River, something in her hand shimmered at him. She thrust it upwards into the man's chin, spraying blood from the wound. His body went limp, loosening his grasp, River kicked off of him towards Bullett.

Bullett had to calculate quickly, with her rate of descent he'd catch her but they'd both hit the ground. She probably couldn't survive it. He glanced back towards Guy, still not close enough but it was a better choice than falling. As she approached, Bullett jerked hard on the chain pulling towards the floor Guy was on. He released the chain and caught River, throwing her towards Guy.

Guy ran forward, having to jump over the large gap in the floor to catch her, and disappeared into the hole with her in hand. Bullett slid to a stop a second later on the same floor. As soon as he regained his footing a bullet struck him in the chest. Looking towards the man that shot him, he pulled the knife from his stomach and threw it at him. The knife, already slick with blood, sunk into the man's abdomen, dropping him where he stood. He clutched his stomach, writhing in his final moments.

Shift watched Guy drop to the floor below, he headbutted the man he had been grappling and focused enough to drop through the floor beneath him.. He fell to ground below, crouching to absorb the impact. Standing in the midsts of the shattered chandelier he searched for Guy in the chaos. Spotting him in the middle of kicking a man in the throat, a young girl in his arms, Shift didn't hesitate to assist.

He knelt and pulled the rifle from his back, aiming down the sights at the officers behind Guy. In short, narrow, bursts the men in the least protective gear were targeted first. He then focused on the armored ones, prioritizing exposed extremities over fatal damage.

Guy could hear the bodies dropping behind him as he continued to fight with only his legs. He kicked just above the knee of a man, snapping the bone, followed by a knee thrust into his chest. The man fell and turned to crawl away, Guy was about to stomp on his spine when the barrel of a gun pressed against his forehead. Shift was reaching to reload and watched as the man's finger pressed to the trigger, he wasn't going to make it in time.

Guy was able to duck just as the first bullet left the chamber but the fully automatic gun angled in his direction. He tried to dash away, but the man whose leg remained in awkward angles grabbed him by the ankle to hold him in place. Shift slid the new magazine into the chamber, praying he was fast enough.

As the gun turned towards Guy and River, a masked body hit the man, knocking him off his feet. Glancing up, Guy saw Bullett standing above the hole in the ceiling, fighting off attackers. He wrapped a chain around one's throat and swung him over his shoulder, throwing him through the hole like a slingshot. The flailing man barely had time to scream before he hit the floor on top of the other two bodies.

With a thumbs up, Bullett disappeared into the hail of gunfire. Guy stomped the ankle of the man holding him then hoisted River over his shoulder and ran towards Shift. Gunfire whizzed past him from both sides as Shift took out anyone targeting his ally. Guy continued past Shift, running through the broken glass and still cowering bodies of civilians.

Shift worked his way backwards, still firing on anyone moving. They were now only against a handful of people, mostly wounded, but backup would surely be on its way soon. Guy slid over the countertop of the lobby main desk with Shift right behind him. Only feet from the desk, a lone bullet passed through his leg. Losing his footing, he fell to the ground. He continued to fire from his back, using his good leg and spare hand to push himself backwards. He bumped into the desk, and leaned against it for leverage to push himself up. Guy reached over the desk, pulling Shift over by the back of his shirt.

Dropping to the ground, all three pressed against the desk for protection. River had tears rolling down her face but refused to cry aloud, she understood who they both were without their explanation. She also understood how bad the situation was without the use of her powers. She hoped Bullett was ok. She could feel his mixture of emotions nearby but his mind was almost blank.

Above them Bullett was fighting exhaustion, he could barely shape the metal in his hand much less fight off the seven or so men left. Surrounded by men, he kept the hole in the floor behind him. This was used to his disadvantage as he now had nowhere to go. Surrounded, the men stopped using guns and the fight turned into a brawl. A fist hit him in the stomach while another one hit his eye. He was knocked onto his back by a kick from someone in the middle. His head bounced hard before resting just on the edge of the floor, dangling above the drop onto a glass covered floor.

Behind him a helicopter lowered into view, a mounted machine gun started firing from it through the windows. Three men were shredded by the rapid fire before the rest could dive for cover. Bullett lay prone on his back watching upside down as they opened fire indiscriminately on anyone moving. The gun tracked one man that ran opposite the majority, taking a few shots to both legs, he fell to the ground. Reaching an arm out to drag himself forward the kill shots came in, pelting his torso and exposed head.

The gun then turned towards the rest hiding behind walls and in cubicles. The line of fire passed inches over Bullett, the heat from the passing ammunition almost burning his flesh. He couldn't take his eyes from the helicopter, hovering like death outside the building. With little warning an explosion ripped through the cockpit, a trail of smoke lead from the impact to a man in a blood soaked mask wielding a grenade launcher.

The aircraft rocked away slightly before another explosion tilted it back towards the building. A second shot, fired from the ground, hit it on the broad side ensuring fatal damage to its occupants. Unmanned, the helicopter was a slave to physics as it crashed through the wall. Propeller still pulling, it tore through stone and glass losing pieces of itself along the way. Bullett had just enough time to drag himself into the hole before it passed overhead.

In the lobby the officers ran for cover once the first explosion hit. They dove behind vehicles and prepared for the worst. Guy could see small parts of the events transpiring on the floor above through the hole in the ceiling. When Bullett started falling he was already on the other side of the counter sprinting towards him. He realized halfway there he wouldn't make it in time to catch him. Glancing back he noticed River dropping down from the counter following behind him.

He turned back just in time to see Bullett disappear behind the chandelier, hitting the ground with a sickening thud. The whole building shook as the helicopter forced its way through. Guy looked back to River, she was oblivious to the building falling around her. Guy was conflicted, should he run to the child to get her out of harm's way or go and check on his friend who was most likely dead? He froze, dropping to his knees he gripped his face with a distorted mixture of pleasure and pain in his eyes.

River stopped when Bullett hit the ground, she couldn't hear his mind. She knew what that meant, at this point she had experienced death enough to know what it was a sign of. Above her the helicopter's fuel tanks ignited, an explosion ripped through several floors above, took out the wall beside and dropped the floor beneath it. River and Guy were both knocked to the ground by the concussive blast. Dazed, River looked up to see the body of the aircraft dropping towards her.

Shift appeared from behind her, grabbing her and pulling her away before the helicopter crashed into view, its burnt and broken body smoldering. Guy rolled out from under large chunks of flooring, it rained down like table-sized hail. It didn't stop falling. More and more the pieces were getting larger and harder to evade. It took Guy a few more dodges to realize the building was collapsing. Walls tilted as they were relieved of their burden, dropping everything to the ground below. Outside, people jumped from windows in a vain attempt to save themselves. With a heave, everything folded in on itself. Dust, papers and bodies poured both in and from the bank to the ground below. It only took seven seconds for the final collapse. Metal, glass, and blood lay bare in the smoking pile of architecture.

Two streets away in a van outfitted with computers and communication equipment, an officer watched the event from several monitors in front of him. Once the building settled he waited several minutes before grabbing a radio.

"Red to Leon."

"This better be good news."

"The building has fallen and no sign of the target sir. It appears he died in the building."

"Excellent, keep six men on watch for the next 24 hours just in case. No one leaves that building alive."

"No one sir? I thought we just had one target."

"I said no one, I don't care if it's your own fucking grandma on a stretcher. NO ONE!"

The radio had a burst of static before he sat it down.

He looked at a clipboard of staff members involved, at this point he didn't even know who was even still alive. The entire thing had gotten completely out of hand. If they had known the bank was being robbed maybe it would have gone differently. But such is the curse of their line of work, there was no such thing as a standard situation for them. He threw the clipboard to the floor in a rage.

"Uh Red… we have a… situation."

A nervous voice called over the radio. He snatched the radio up and had to forcibly keep himself from yelling.

"What, at this point, could possibly be a situation?"

The telltale sounds of the radio exchanging hands then a very familiar voice came through his speakers.

"Red, this is Theodore Grayson, President of the United States, I'm going to need to use your men. There's a chance my daughter is in that bank and we're going to get her back as well as any survivors."

The officer stood dumbfounded, this was most definitely a situation and one he had no control over. He stammered back a quick yes sir and forwarded communications to the President at his command. A knock came from the van door, he opened it to see nothing but a silenced gun barrel in his face.

"Leon?"

"You're services are no longer needed."

The man dropped to the floor, a hole in the middle of his forehead. Leon straightened his tie and flattened his suit. He smiled to himself, the game was more interesting by the second. A limo with tinted windows pulled up, the driver quickly got out and opened the door for him. Leon sat on the plush leather back seat, where a freshly poured glass of scotch waited for him.

"Where to?" The driver asked as he retook his seat.

"The nearest airport, I have business to attend to. Were you instructed to pour me a drink?"

"N..no sir, I just heard you liked scotch and I..."

"Well done lad, you've just earned yourself a promotion."

"Um, sir I don't actually work for you."

"You do now, now drive."

"Y..yes sir."

Leon swirled the glass beneath his nose before taking a sip.

"I can already tell these... *children* of Iris are going to be quite problematic." He said with a clinched jaw.

He watched the bent reflections on the window convey a distorted scenery to him. The lights and smoke shrunk in the distance. He smiled, he made his first move since the game started. He wondered to himself what their next move would be.

293

Epilogue

Raven tapped her foot while nervously twisting the ends of her bangs. The airport security man in front of her was looking over her laptop, holding it precariously. For the third time he flipped it upside down using his palms on the corners. Her foot came to an abrupt stop.

"Please don't drop that. My entire life is on that hard drive."

Standing at only 5'5", she wasn't very intimidating in stature, but her emerald eyes seemed to glow with a piercing intensity that contrasted her jet black hair.

The uniformed man eyed her over the rim of his glasses for a moment before placing it onto the conveyer belt to be scanned. Following her laptop, Raven quickly emptied her pockets into a basket and stepped through a metal detector. She nearly screamed the third time she was made to walk through the detector. Security ran a metal wand over her a few times before it beeped, indicating a loan penny deep in the recesses of her pocket to be the culprit of her whole ordeal.

Finally, laptop secured in a bag on her hip, she was able to let out a sigh of relief. She lined up with the other passengers to board her flight, biting at the string hanging from the hood of her jacket. She was hungry, she always got hungry when she was anxious. She looked around spotting a vending machine on a far wall, grabbing a few bills crumbled in her pocket, she proceeded to smooth them on her way to the machine.

Staring at the grossly over-priced candy, she talked herself out of an energy bar in favor of a chocolate bar. Today was the start of her trip to comic-con, she could pamper herself a little.

Returning to the line, chocolate already halfway gone, she pulled out her ticket to look it over one more time. A flight to San Diego, just three short hours away. She considered either an anime marathon or a long nap. Sleeping was out of the question, she was way too excited to let the foul hands of the sandman sully her energy. Besides, she had been saving a small series specifically for this occasion.

Behind her, an old man grumbled, his sputtering cough and incoherent muttering both normal and uncomfortable in crowded public spaces. Raven quickly glanced at him, noting the matted beard and multiple layers of stained coats. She secretly hoped he wouldn't be sitting next to her, his odor alone was enough to have her reconsider her trip.

As the line inched forward, she drummed her fingers along the bag at her hip, anything to take her mind off of the repugnant smell enveloping her. A few minutes of aimless fidgeting and it was her turn. The ticket agent smiled as he took her ticket in exchange for a receipt. With a quick half bow, Raven turned and hustled down the bridge to the plane.

Inside, she squeezed past other passengers, finding her seat next to a window. She gazed out to the sunlit wing, light glinting like liquid off the frame. The large turbine engine hung beneath it like ripe fruit. She briefly pondered the physics of flight.

A wall of putrid smell washed over her, snapping her out of her curious state. Skulking down the aisle, the bearded man pointed to various parts of the plane and cackled to himself. Raven held her breath when the man paused next to her, momentarily making eye contact before continuing past her. His rattling breath and milky eyes would surely haunt her dreams. It took another 10 minutes before the final passenger boarded. Raven reached for her bag beneath her when a chime rang through the cabin.

"Ladies and gentlemen. The "Fasten Seatbelt" sign has been turned by the Captain. Please stow your carry-on luggage underneath your seat or in an overhead bin."

Raven grabbed her seatbelt and clicked it into place. With arms resting on both armrests, she quietly thanked the gods for the empty seat next to her. She looked out of her window and watched as the turbines slowly spun to life. The plane eventually taxied down the runway and soon they climbed towards the clouds.

From the air, Raven looked past the wings of the plane to the ground below. The cities beneath them shrank and meshed together forming a brown and gray grid amongst the green patches of land. She momentarily dreamed of soaring amongst the clouds, feeling the crisp air against her skin and wind in her hair with arms outstretched towards the fluffy pillows in the sky.

The picturesque view could only hold her attention for a limited time however, her thoughts soon turned to her laptop which held a whole new adventure to experience. Another chime in the cabin and a new message came over the speakers.

"Ladies and gentlemen, the Captain has turned off the "Fasten Seatbelt" sign and, you are free to move around the cabin."

That was all Raven needed to hear, she quickly retrieved her bag and slid out her laptop. Sliding the tray out from the seat in front of her, it only took seconds before she was typing in her password and pulling up her new anime. Headphones in and opening credits rolling, she had to fight her inner fangirl not to squeal at the adorable half bird ninja.

Raven was thoroughly engrossed from the second the opening song started, and the world around her was all but forgotten. The spunky feathered girl sang as she awkwardly walked through the streets of feudal Japan. Dark shadowy ninjas appeared from behind buildings and bushes in an attempt to ambush her. With a grand gesture, she swung her feathery wings in a wide arc, throwing quills in every direction. Every foe was dispatched in time to the music and the girl continued on her merry way.

Raven's seat lurched forward, almost throwing her into the screen of her laptop. Her first instinct was turbulence but, a quick glance out the window showed no signs of strong winds. With another heavy bump she turned to look behind her, the person directly behind her was standing up pointing a finger towards the gross smelling man. Who was grinning with bright yellow teeth.

Raven shrugged and went back to her anime, whatever problem they were having she was glad she wasn't in the middle of it. The avian ninja in front of her was now soaring in the clouds with samurai cats using kites to give chase. Even the bad guys in this show were super cute and she just knew the bright pink one was going to be a main character too.

By her third episode, Raven had her knees pulled up in front of her with her arms wrapped around them for the sake of having something to hug. Her inner giggles almost escaped from her lips a few times so, she took to biting her knee as a coping mechanism. A momentary flash of light in her peripheral distracted her from the most adorable fight known to man, outside her window a jet flew no more than 20 yards away from the wing.

She watched as he pointed towards the ground, looking towards the front of the plane. Due to air traffic laws she knew there must be a big problem, she paused the show and turned to see if anyone else noticed the jet. As soon as the noise in her headphones stopped, a bombardment of yelling hit her ears.

Three passengers and a flight attendant were all struggling with the homeless man, he just stood there as though he didn't notice their weight pressing against him at all. He tilted his head back and looked to the light fixtures in the ceiling above him. He mumbled a few words and lifted his arm, finger pointing straight ahead at an empty row of seats behind Raven.

There was 3 full seconds of complete silence, an unnatural quiet that made Raven go from confused to fearful in a serene instinctual way. The silence was immediately swallowed by the sound of a large section of the plane collapsing upon itself. Metal screeched and wind howled as a 10 foot wide hole ripped outward from the plane. Raven reached for her seatbelt but the luxury of time wasn't on her side.

The plane became unstable with the gaping wound in its frame and the wing on Raven's side snapped like a twig. The spinning wing dug into the plane and tore its way down the side, destroying part of the tail of the plane before falling towards the earth. The peeling of metal barely missed Raven but, the damage done was enough to dismantle the plane.

Raven's screams joined the chorus of other passengers as they, and their belongings, were sucked from the plane and thrown into the sky. Raven could only look to the jet above her, missiles armed and thrusters flaring as they fired upon the plane.

Caught in a spin, Raven struggled to stay conscious as the earth circled the outer edges of her vision. Everything started to blur and the rushing winds felt like daggers stabbing her all over. Somewhere beneath her, her laptop continued to play the ending credits to the anime.

Gasping for breath and trying to steady herself, Raven outstretched her arms. The stabbing sensation worsened, and Raven felt as though she'd be dead long before she hit the fast approaching ground. Her spine felt as though it had snapped and was being pulled out of her back with a meat hook. Raven's descent stabilized and her vision returned to normal. Facing down now, she could clearly see the trees fast approaching, only it felt as though she was falling slower than before.

People and debris soon began to pass her in their free fall, the wind was starting to feel less harsh and the stinging sensation was almost entirely gone. A rustling sound filled her ears, she turned her head towards the source to see hundreds of feathers protruding from her back like wings. Her movement caused her to lean, sending her flying to the side much faster than her fall. She quickly leaned the other way, reaching a slow descent once again.

A loud, ominous groaning above her took her attention away from her new feathered appendages. The fully destroyed plane was raining scraps of metal and flames around her. A burning sensation started in her stomach and worked its way up into her back. With a cannon like explosion, Raven shot forth at incredible speeds. Leaving the burning debris behind her, the forest blended into a single shade of green as she gained momentum.

Inside the jet, a pilot fidgeted with the controls in front of him. His helmet already soaked in sweat, he called back to the Tactical Operations Center.

"Demon3, this is Howard-505, requesting additional support. Unidentified female flying due east. Escort failed, target destroyed."

"Howard-505, Demon-3 responding. Come again, you said female is flying? Any identifiable traits of the aircraft?"

"Negative Demon-3, it is a girl… with wings and some sort of propulsion device. Looks like a miniature thruster mounted on her back."

"Can you repeat? This is not an aircraft…"

"… it is a girl Demon-3. A flying girl."

"Stand by."

The pilot slowed to match the girl's speed, trying to get his reticle aligned on her. She was much smaller than another aircraft.

"Howard-505 you are clear to engage. I repeat engage."

Screaming, Raven was too confused to think straight. Feathers flying behind her with a trail of smoke in her wake, the jet that had previously escorted them was now tracing her path. Missiles fired at Raven, whizzing past her and exploding in front of her. Raven tried to halt herself from hitting the cloud of flames. As her body turned upright, she arched skywards like a rocket. Her airborne adversary fired a spray of bullets in a sweeping arc behind her. She instinctively shied away from it, one wing dipped slightly and she rolled to the side. As the storm of bullets tracked her, she dipped and rolled back and forth. Getting more adept with each movement. The firing stopped abruptly, she glanced over her shoulder to see the aircraft gaining on her. With a swing of her feet, she gained altitude but lost momentum.

The jet gave chase, firing again with two missiles this time. As they shot past her, Raven dove down, she was getting used to flying. With a tilt, she shot to the side as the jet streamed past her. She was surprised at how quickly she was learning to fly. It was fairly simple, lean with the shoulders and the body would follow. Hair whipping in the wind, she darted towards the trees below. Behind her, the jet pulled a sharp turn to give chase.

Raven sped towards the tree tops, aware of fires burning in several patches around her. Using smoke for cover, she took a nosedive through branches before she could be shot at again. She crashed through branches and limbs in the least graceful way possible before slamming into a tree. The tree shook violently at the impact, raining sticks and leaves to the earth below. Raven collapsed to the ground, wings outstretched and jaw clenched.

From her spot on the ground, she watched the clouds roll by as smoke billowed behind her. The jet streaked by, shooting missiles and a hail of bullets wildly into the trees beyond. The aircraft circled the area, shooting at the slightest sign of movement. Raven couldn't help but smile, this was just like the beginning of an anime…

Made in the USA
Charleston, SC
29 March 2016